Murder in Carmel

A novel by

Arlene Grace

Stely Publishing
A division of Stely LLC
© Copyright 2014

ISBN-13: 9780991453429
ISBN-10: 0991453425

Author's photography by: Cari Baun
Library of Congress Cataloguing-in-Publications
Data has been applied for.

This book is dedicated to my three
Beautiful children, with all my love.

1

Carlota Dominguez parked her car near the entrance to her art gallery on Ocean Avenue in Carmel. Carmel by the Sea is the kind of place where nothing ever happens. It's a romantic, picturesque little town located on California's central coast, on the edge of the Pacific Ocean. The locals here enjoy a quiet life in a laid-back community whose favorite pastime is picnicking and opening a bottle of wine in the evening at the water's edge, and breaking out into applause at sunset. Many of its visitors are sophisticated shoppers who also frequent exclusive stores on Rodeo Drive and New York's Fifth Avenue. Ocean Avenue starts at Highway One and ends at the edge of the sand at Carmel Beach.

The street is lined with quaint little shops, restaurants, and art galleries. At night, the trees light up with little lights that give it that perfect ambiance. Carlota and her brother Gustavo moved to Carmel fifteen years ago from Argentina by way of Los Angeles. They were an odd pair; neither of them ever married. She is tall and awkward and the spitting image of Mamie Eisenhower. He is a short, stout little man who has an awful habit of spitting when he speaks if he's nervous or excited. They share a house on Carmelo Street. They purchased it with some of the money they had received from their father's estate. Leaving Argentina had seemed like the right thing to do at the time.

Having lost their mother years before, they had no other family left to speak of, just an older uncle who was senile and a couple of distant cousins. Their dad had some undesirable connections to some of the relatives and families, descendents of the Nazi era who had relocated there after the fall of Berlin. Carlota and Gustavo weren't crazy about that, but had enjoyed the benefits of running around with a very wealthy crowd and had developed very expensive taste. Their father dabbled in art and had many connections, both good and bad. They had decided to make a new start in a country with a more stable form of government, and had made the move after receiving permanent resident status.

This was the beginning of a very busy week for them. It was the week in August that hosted the Concours d'Elegance in Pebble Beach. *The* event of the year. It has been an annual charity event since 1950. There are many to do's around town. Car auctions, races, parties, and of course, the showing of the rarest and most beautiful cars that are invited to appear on the famed eighteenth fairway of Pebble Beach Golf Links. Lovers of art and technology congregate to see the cars and spend their money all over town. This was Carlota's and Gustavo's busiest week of the year, and the time during which they made most of their money.

Carlota had sent out more than one thousand invitations to previous visitors, clients, and celebrities from all over the world hoping to engage them during an open house that was to take place on Wednesday evening at the gallery.

As she slammed her car door and hurried to open early, she was greeted by Lindsay Reed. Carlota had hired the former Miss Carmel to work part time during this week, primarily for her looks. She needed an attractive reason for visitors to come in and take a look at the display of paintings and sculptures they were featuring. She was a tall five foot, nine-inch brunette with an expensive boob job that would make even your mama turn her head and look. Her main duty will be to stand by the door and be seen as passersby glanced in the direction of the gallery. But she was also going to be passing out drinks and mingling with the un-escorted men attending the open house. She was a sweet young thing who had a natural knack for spotting wealthy men, and that was about the only gift she had, aside from her looks.

"Lindsay, why are you here so early? You aren't due until noon today," Carlota asked as she turned the key in the door to open it.

"Well, my car had to go in the shop and I got a ride from a friend. She was on her way to work, so I thought I would just come in and hang out. Hope its okay."

"Sure, just grab the duster and get a head start at giving everything a quick once over before we get anyone in here."

Carlota turned on the lights and ran into her office.

She was on edge. With the planning of Wednesday's event and everything they had going on, they needed this to be a very beneficial week.

Gustavo had started gambling again and had gone through all of their money. Their house was about to go into foreclosure, and they were two months behind on the rent for the gallery. She had managed to talk the owner into giving her until the end of this month. She assured him that she would be able to pay him in full as well as in advance a few months as a way of showing appreciation for his understanding.

Carlota felt like killing Gustavo for getting mixed up in online gambling again. She thought that his staying home was a good sign because he wasn't jetting off to Vegas where he usually went to squander their cash and get laid. Now in his late forties and not exactly God's gift to women, he had to spend a little to get a little. He stood at only four feet ten inches and he had scoliosis that had turned him into a bit of a hunch back. He was balding and wasn't always in the cleanest condition. But he was an art genius. He could paint like anyone's business. Gustavo had the ability to recreate and duplicate masterpieces to look like any work of art hanging in the museums. He had a gift few people are born with. Making his living doing portraits, he would spend the time when he was not contracted, teaching at Monterey Peninsula College and eating canned sardines. That didn't help with his dental hygiene. He hated using a toothbrush.

Carlota had banned him from going to the gallery during this week. She had a plan to make a lot of money very fast. And she was making him contribute to her plan in order to make up for putting them in such an awful predicament. He was going to have to retrieve art that was being transported to the area. She'd made arrangements to sell the painting to one of their shady contacts in Argentina for a lot of money. Getting art into that country isn't like bringing it into the U.S. The customs agents there were easily paid off, and getting it through was a piece of cake. Getting it into the U.S., well that was a different story.

2

Italy 1940

Carlo Astor and his family ran a private school for boys in Milan, Italy. They were Italian, but no one knew they were Jewish. They had settled there in 1935, two years after Germany fell to Hitler. More than thirty thousand Jews hid secretly in Italy. Many appeared to be Nazi sympathizers and were card-carrying members of the German Reich. Although Mussolini proclaimed hatred against Jews, Italians had no personal hatred toward them. For the most part, they were protected from the Nazis for many years. Many Jews fled to Italy at the beginning, changed their names, and went on with their lives, not realizing how big and out of control the Nazi reign would become in Europe.

The Astors and their two sons were educators and later also became some of the many who helped Jewish families in the escape from Hitler's terror camps.

As things progressed and the Nazis hold became stronger and bigger, the Astors began aiding many families by assisting them with the connection they had at the Vatican, after the election of Pope Pius XII, whose appointment was greatly opposed by Hitler and his regime. Pope Pius XII was quite outspoken about his opinions of Hitler, and made no secret of his criticisms of their cruelty toward Jews and many other races.

In exchange for helping them obtain transit visas from the Pope as members of an "Apostolic Delegation," families would pay the Astors with jewels, silver, gold, valuable coins, and art. As many of them were affluent, they had these items to offer in lieu of payment, keeping the cash they could smuggle to aid them in settling where ever they were to end up.

Cardinal Eugenio Maggio was one of Pope Pius' right-hand men and the connection from Astors to the Vatican. He traveled to Milan by train from Rome twice a month and aided the transportation of the "Apostolic Delegates" to Vatican City. There, they were offered asylum until passage could be arranged to England. From that point, they were on their own.

Many settled in England, but most arranged to leave Europe all together. A great deal of them traveled to New York and began their own community along with the many others who at that time that were emigrating from other countries.

Angela Marcello was a cousin of Carlo Astor. She had married into a wealthy Italian family that owned a bank in Milan. It was a new bank, but one that seemed to be thriving. Carlo approached Angela's husband about using of one of his vaults under the bank property. He had assured most of the families that he would do what he could to hold many of their prized possessions until they could re-claim them. After all, he couldn't keep anything in their modest home, or it would be a dead giveaway to some of the neighbors who were beginning to turn and spy on others in exchange for food or clothing for their families. Food had begun to be rationed and necessity and survival kicked in after a while.

Michaelo would help Carlo place these items in the back of his car and take them to the bank in the dead of night. They would back the car up into one of the large storage rooms they used at the school, and quietly drive them there. The bank had a back delivery driveway that sloped underground. There, the two of them would put the valuables in the vault and Michaelo hid the key. No one else in the family knew what was in that large vault. Not even his wife Angela.

One evening in August 1943, there was a knock on the door of the Astor home. Louie Astor, the youngest son went to open it and the house was immediately invaded by Nazi soldiers looking for hidden art. Someone had turned the family in. Josef Goebbels was one of Hitler's propaganda ministers. He demanded to see where the hidden art was being kept. Hitler considered any work of art by anyone other than German artists to be "degenerate art," and had ordered it burned. When the family was unable to produce any of it, they were taken outside and shot in the head one by one.

Michaelo never disclosed the contents of that vault. He died with the secret that was hidden inside. The bank passed on to the next generations, and it remained closed ... until one afternoon.

3

Carlota called Lindsay into her office. "Lindsay, I want you to take my Black AMX card and go across the street to Saks. Go to the ladies department and ask for Dolores. She's going to help you pick out a cocktail dress for Wednesday night. She's a stylist friend of mine. I spoke with her last night and she knows what I have in mind. Run along now."

"Gee, thanks Miss Carlota. I was going to wear something I all ready had, but this is great! Thank you!"

Carlota watched Lindsay as she crossed the street. She had a lot riding on this Wednesday night's open house. She had borrowed a ton of money already on that card to make the event work. The catering company, the liquor, she had even hired a bartender and waiter to help with the festivities. She was a nervous wreck! Sick and tired of having to bail Gustavo out all the time was bad enough, but now he had practically ruined them. He had squandered the money in their joint account for the gallery, and now again she was left to clean up his mess.

Once she was sure Lindsay was far enough away, Carlota locked the door to the gallery and went into her office. She was waiting for a call that was about to come in. It was now 11:00 A.M. and right on time, the phone rang.

"Senora Carlota?" said the voice with an Italian accent on the other end.

"Si, it's me, is this Luigi?" she asked.

"Si, it is Luigi. I want to confirm that the money you wired has been received at the bank, and the item you will be receiving has left and is on its way to you. It will arrive tonight at the Monterey Airport at around 8:30 just like we agreed. Now it's all up to you."

"Thank you Luigi. I'll handle things on my end. Perhaps we can do business again."

"Perhaps," said Luigi.

Carlota heard a click on the other end. The conversation had been short, but all that was necessary had been said. Now, her nerves really set in. Her heart began to race and she had to take deep breaths to keep from having a panic attack. She couldn't let anyone see her like this. She needed to get to work to make sure everything went as planned. The thought of having to go broke in this community would bring her shame and ruin her reputation, not to mention her pride. She couldn't let it happen, and she was willing to do just about anything.

Three weeks before this, Carlota had received a strange phone call from the man she had just spoken to. Luigi said he got her name from a family member who had known her father, and who knew she and Gustavo were art dealers in Carmel. How convenient their location was. He had a friend who was looking to sell a piece of art that had been hidden since World War II and was a masterpiece painted by Rembrandt. He didn't elaborate as to how his friend had come across it, but was hoping she might still have some of her father's 'old' connections, and would be able to help sell it, or perhaps would be interested in purchasing it herself, and then sell it on the black market for a good price.

The call had come weeks after she discovered that they were broke. At any other time, she would have had no part of this. But having been approached at this particular time, she thought it was the answer to all of her problems. She'd received an email with a picture of the painting, and it looked legitimate. She'd agreed to purchase it on her own and had wired the $100,000 to an Italian bank in Milan. But putting things in motion was tearing her up inside. The money had come from her personal retirement account. It's all she had left. It was certainly a gamble, but she felt she could sell it for five times that.

Carlota called Gustavo and told him the package would be landing tonight and it was now or never. It was up to him to go and retrieve it. She knew he wasn't very reliable, but she certainly wasn't going to do it. She had done enough. He's the one who had gotten them into this mess and he had to help get them out.

4

Milan, Italy, one month earlier

Roberto Marcello was the middle son of Paolo Marcello. The family had lived in Milan, Italy for many generations. They were the owners of one of the oldest and largest banks in Italy. The oldest branch was right there in Milan.

His father Paolo had recently decided to retire and enjoy his life a little more. After all, he had been widowed and raised his three boys alone. He felt that it was his time now to travel and enjoy his hobby of collecting and restoring old classic automobiles. That as well as entering into a long term relationship that he was enjoying with a beautiful woman from Carmel, California. Victoria Rite was born in Charleston, South Carolina. He adored her southern accent and worshiped her charm and her body. Unlike many women his age, Victoria had a beautiful figure and creamy smooth white skin. He had met her through her brother—in-law who is in the banking business while she was visiting him and her sister the year before. Paolo had fallen completely under her spell and was happier than he had ever been.

Roberto was Paolo's favorite son. He was charming and very good looking, but too much of a womanizer. He was very much of a playboy. He loved women and had a reputation for breaking hearts and having the best of everything. He had no concept of money. Now, dad had given him this bank branch to run and earn his own living. He was to take an agreed upon draw for a salary, and start to grow up. Dad felt it was time for him to settle down and be more responsible.

Bored one rainy afternoon, Roberto decided to check out the bank and go exploring. He hadn't spent much time there and had only faint memories of visiting different areas of the bank with his dad and grandfather.

The tall huge building was built in the early 1920s. Outside it had massive pillars and inside there were marble columns and marble floors. The windows were draped with velvet curtains. There were many teller cages adorned with bright shiny brass which was always maintained immaculately. The lobby had huge velvet couches and fresh flowers were always in the vases that were placed everywhere. There were two small offices in the front for business banking. In the back, away from view, was the office Roberto now claimed as his own. It had been used by his father and the other members of his family before him. It was quite large and very ornate.

He'd only been in charge of the bank for one month and didn't like staying inside all day. He was always looking for an excuse to leave. But it was a miserable day and going out would only mean he had to deal with bad weather and even worse, traffic. Italians aren't noted for being the world's most patient drivers. And in bad weather, their patience was even shorter. It was always better to stay off the roads on days like today.

Roberto hadn't really paid much attention to his new office. His father must have just figured that Roberto had poked around over the years, and would know all there was to know about the place. He never really told him about what was in there. He decided to see what was in a built-in cabinet across from his desk. He walked over and opened the double doors. Inside, he found there were many small drawers that were locked and had small key holes. Wondering what they contained, he looked through his desk drawers. In the back of the bottom drawer, he found a set of small keys on an old ring. He walked over to see if these keys opened the small cabinet drawers, and they fit. Inside of the small compartments were large keys that were tagged with numbers. He put a couple in his jacket pocket and went into the bank vault. There were many safety deposit boxes, but none had the numbers that coincided with these keys.

He found this to be very curious. *"What do these large numbered keys belong to"?* he wondered. This was certainly intriguing. He made up his mind that he was going to find out.

Later that evening, when everyone had left the bank, Roberto set out to explore. He had been giving thought to his dilemma and remembered that once when he was a small child, his grandfather had taken him to the bank when it was closed. He was told to sit on a chair in the lobby and not move.

"If you are a good boy, we'll go to buy you a nice gelato." he had said.

Grandfather had disappeared down the hall from his big office. Being the curious little boy that he was, after grandfather had been gone a few minutes, Roberto tiptoed down the hall to see what he was up to. He noticed at the end of that long hallway, there was a thick red velvet curtain that had been drawn exposing a very heavy large opened door. He could hear his grandfather walking around at a distance, so he snuck a peek inside. There was set of stairs that led to a large dark cold space. He went down several steps, and saw what looked like many more heavy doors that were closed.

Being afraid of getting caught and wanting that gelato, he ran back and sat on the chair as if nothing had ever happened. A few minutes later, grandpa reappeared and off they went. Having had no interest in what had just happened, he never gave it a second thought. Nothing was ever said between them about that. And Roberto had forgotten all about that day until now. It was all coming back.

Roberto walked slowly to the end of the long hallway, to see if what he was remembering had been a dream, or if it was real. Sure enough, the heavy red velvet curtain was still there. No one would have ever given it a second thought. You would have just figured it covered a window, or was just hung there for decoration. But he just knew he had find out if the door was still there, and if it was, he was going get behind it to see what was down there. He wondered if the keys he had found in those small drawers would open the secrets at the bottom of the stairs.

Roberto found the curtain pull and drew it open, revealing that same heavy thick door he remembered. It was re-enforced with steel bars that ran through it laterally as well as horizontally. But now he had another dilemma: he needed *that* key.

Back to the cabinet he went. He opened every small cabinet drawer looking for something large enough to fit. Finally, he found one that was not tagged with a number. He ran back to the door and slowly placed the large key in the key hole, and it turned. He was in! The door was heavy as he pulled it open. He swung it all the way open, and then was afraid of having it close behind him. So he went to get a chair from his office and set it up against the door. It was dark; it smelled very dingy and musty. The wooden steps creaked under his feet as he walked down toward the mysterious darkness.

When he got to the bottom of the stairs, he saw a cord hanging from the ceiling with a bulb at the end. He pulled it and a small light went on. He could see seven large doors similar to the one he had just opened. They looked like they hadn't been opened in years. As he walked further, he found an old light switch. Being afraid of getting electrocuted, he took off his leather shoe and pushed it up. It worked and the room was dimly lit.

Roberto was astonished at what was hidden under his family bank. No one had ever spoken about anything like this to him or to each other. You would have thought that now that he was in charge, his father would have mentioned something to his about all of this. Perhaps his father didn't think he was quite ready to be told the bank's secret just yet.

Roberto reached into his pocket and found three of the keys he had retrieved from the small cabinet doors. One was marked "3," another "4," and the last one "6."

Walking slowly to the first one, he inserted the corresponding key and took a deep breath. The key turned and he heard a click. As he swung the door open. A rush of very musty cold air hit him in the face. As he looked inside, all he could see was old furniture piled as high as the ceiling. There were also old musty curtains and an old sewing machine. Surely some of this stuff by now would be considered antiques, but nothing that would interest him. He wondered if this was stuff that belonged to his family. He closed the large door and locked it as it had been before.

He then made his way to door number 4. Again, he placed the key in the hole and it turned. This time, he had to give the door a bit of a tug. There was nothing inside. It looked as though it had contained items packed in some old remaining trunks at one time. But now, the trunks were empty and the smell was awful. So he locked it and moved on the door marked 6.

This door was at the end of the room and seemed wider than the others. This one as well as door 7 were the same and were on a different wall.

The key went in, it twisted, and he gave the door a pull. Roberto stood nearly frozen, as what he found inside took his breath away. The very huge storage room contained rows and rows of paintings and sculptures. He had a feeling they were all of great value, otherwise, why would his family have stored them for such a long time and in great secrecy? This question baffled him.

Stepping inside, he didn't know what to look at first. Some of the paintings had tags with family names like Schwartz, Levine, and Hoffman. He then explored more, looking inside the many old wooden boxes that were stacked almost to the ceiling. Inside, he found old yellow envelopes also marked with family names. They contained antique jewelry and hundreds of very old gold and silver coins.

As he further examined some of the paintings, he saw many famous names he recognized and some that he didn't. He was no art aficionado, but knew they were sitting of some very valuable things. There were paintings by Matisse, Chagall, and Rembrandt, to name a few. *"Mama Mia!"* he exclaimed. *"This place is sitting on a gold mine!"* But what to do about it was what he had to give some thought to.

5

oberto made a call the very next morning to an old friend of his from the university. They had met in Rome where they had studied finance. He knew this fellow was the kind of fellow who had some questionable connections and might be able to help sell some of these items for money. Now that his father had put him on a generous but limited salary, Roberto had decided to get creative and found that this was a way to maintain his playboy lifestyle. He wouldn't disclose where these things were coming from, he would just say he was "liquidating some of his inheritance to exchange for cash and different investments." He had opened the other lockers and there was more of the same: jewelry, rare books, more coins, and paintings. Roberto had figured out that perhaps everything stored under his family

bank had to have belonged to some of the Jewish families that had either fallen to the Holocaust or that had
entrusted his great-grandfather for safe keeping until
they returned. Surely no one was going to come after
them now. He may as well sell a little bit here and a little
bit there, just enough so he could continue the lifestyle he
was known for and put off some of that settling down his
father was so anxious to see him do. If he played his cards
right, no one would know. After all, he didn't think anyone in the family was aware of those storage lockers, and
surely his father would never suspect anything missing.
He just had to be smart about it.

Roberto and his college friend Vincente Abbatecola
were the kind of friends who understood one another.
They were both from families with affluence and came
from old money. They were always in trouble together and
always partied in the same circles. Vicente had a side of the
family that was not exactly everyone's favorite. There is
always one or two of those in just about everyone's family.
Vincente had arranged to meet Roberto for supper that
same evening and discuss how to address his old friend's
needs. After exchanging pleasantries and discussing
each other's latest conquests, Roberto told Vicente that
he was looking to sell some family art, and didn't have
any connections. He told him also his dilemma of not
wanting to have his family know he was selling some of
his inheritance at this time. He said he was going to take
the money and invest it in real estate. After telling him
what he wanted to sell was a painting by Matisse, Vicente

said he knew the perfect person. They called a guy named Marco. He met them later that evening at a bar. After Vicente made the introductions, he excused himself as he was expected at a night club and it was late. Marco listened to Roberto and gave him a price. He required ten percent of the sale price to make it happen. Roberto agreed. Roberto told Marco that he would set up two bank accounts in his bank under fictitious names. Marco was to arrange the money be wired to Roberto's bank under the first account, and after it arrived, Roberto would personally transfer Marco's part of the money into the second account and make it available to him without any red tape. Marco asked for a few days to make some calls and put Roberto's number into his cell phone.

Four days later, Roberto's phone rang early in the morning. Marco had contacted someone he knew in Argentina who found him a possible connection in the States. This person couldn't promise that the U.S. contact would be willing to go through with this, but they decided to place a call and take a chance.

Roberto and Marco placed the call to Carlota one evening. The call caught her quite by surprise. She told them she had to think about it before she could give them an answer.

The sale of paintings on the black market was one of the reasons Carlota had decided that she and Gustavo would move. They saw their father get involved with less than reputable people who would buy, sell, or trade art in one form or another with drug lords, crooks, and killers.

That was the one thing she promised herself she would never have anything to do with. But her head was in a vice, and now she found this opportunity the only way out of a very difficult situation. The next day, still unsure she really wanted to go through with this, she waited for Marco to call back. She agreed and they made the arrangements. But how would the painting get to the U.S.? Marco and Roberto couldn't believe their luck. Paolo had just told Roberto that he was going to take his new prized Bugatti to the Concours d'Elegance in California. There was the ride they needed for the Matisse. They would put the painting in the car and no one would be the wiser. After all, who would search an old car for precious art? Drugs maybe, but a dusty old painting?

Roberto went down into to the vault and did exactly as Marco told him to do. He took a box cutter and ever so carefully cut the canvas away from the frame and rolled it up. He met Marco outside the bank and two of them then traveled to the garage where Paolo had the car stored, all ready on a trailer. They knew it wasn't going to be driven for a while.

Roberto watched Marco pick the lock to the garage where Paolo kept his most expensive automobiles. It made them wonder how come there was no alarm. But it was on private property, so it never occurred to Paolo that he would need one.

Roberto showed Marco the car. It was simply amazing! Marco walked around it in awe of the beauty. He then climbed in behind the steering column.

Roberto had rolled up the painting in between two pieces of plastic wrap just as he had been asked to do. Marco took some tools out of the inside of his jacket pocket, and began to remove the steering wheel. This was the perfect place to hide the painting. This car had a very long steering column and only one wire that ran through it. He slid the painting into the column and replaced the steering wheel.

"Finitoa," said Marco and he replaced the tools into his jacket. They hurried back out and locked the door. The car was going to get loaded onto a jet that evening. Paolo had already left for California, and would meet the car there. They placed that call to Carlota. When they got back to the city, they shook hands and parted ways.

Roberto had gotten away with it. He had his cash. Marco had his money. All was good.

6

They say love is lovelier the second time around and it seemed to be just that for Victoria Rite and Paolo Marcello. Victoria had been a widow for many years. Her first husband James had been a Naval officer who died in Greece while they were taking a cruise vacation. He died from an accidental overdose of Viagra while they made love in their cabin one lovely afternoon. James had left her and their daughter Abbey, quite well off. He'd made wise investments as well as having left them a very large trust and, well, some other things. She had spent years traveling all over Europe with a very ritzy crowd. Her sister Violet and brother-in-law Jon lived in Italy. He was in the banking business and they had moved to several cities there. Jon was a forensic accountant who audited banks and was always paid quite generously.

Always at her yoga classes or the dermatologist office getting one treatment or other, Victoria had kept herself quite youthful-looking for someone her age.

Paolo had lost his wife and fourth son during child birth. He had been left to raise their three young sons alone. Everything he did was for his boys. He made sure they always had the best money could buy and gave them the best education. Paolo came from a long line of bank owners. His family owned three of the largest banks in Italy. One day during a conference in Rome, he ran into Jonathan, Victoria's brother-in-law. Victoria and her sister had gone with him to shop and enjoy the sites while he worked.

Jon had invited Paolo to dinner that evening and introduced him to Victoria. He had a hunch they would hit it off: It was love at first sight!

Victoria couldn't keep her eyes off of Paolo all evening. He was strong and handsome and very sophisticated looking. He had dark hair that he combed straight back and big brown eyes. She could see his chest hair peeking out of the top of his silk shirt. That was her biggest turn on! Victoria had a thing for hairy men.

Paolo couldn't take his eyes off of Victoria, either. They talked and laughed all evening. He adored her southern accent. It was almost as if it was just the two of them there. Paolo invited Victoria to go see his antique car collection and to dinner when they returned to Milan. She couldn't say yes fast enough.

That following Saturday afternoon, Paolo picked her up in his Lamborghini and off they went. They drove through the countryside to his estate in the country. The conversation never ended. They shared with one another, the loss of their spouses, and how they'd spent that long period of time since then. They seemed to have so much in common. The timing couldn't have been better. They both now had their hearts open.

Paolo cooked her a lovely dinner in his kitchen. They drank wine all day and all evening, while gazing into each other's eyes the entire time. When dinner was over, they sat on a lovely huge leather couch in his living room in front of a big roaring fire. Paolo had opened a bottle of champagne and poured each of them a glass to toast.

"Bella," he whispered, "if I don't kiss you soon, I will burst."

"Well darlin', let's not have any burstin'. Come here and give me some sugah'". And with that, Victoria leaped toward him and they kissed a long, slow, lingering kiss.

Paolo leaned back onto the couch and pulled Victoria on top. His kisses were soft and tender. Victoria felt him grow beneath her. She opened his shirt and slowly ran her hand down his wonderfully hairy chest, all the way down to feel him, and stroked him gently from top to bottom. Paolo made a slow, long, moaning sound, letting her know he liked it. Paolo grabbed Victoria's back side and started to stroke her. His hands softly went up and down her back. She sat up and slipped her light cotton dress over her head. She hadn't worn a bra that day on purpose. She had wanted to show off her girls. He smiled and cupped her firm breasts with delight at what he saw. They were perky and full.

"Bella, you are beautiful! You are perfect!" He wet his fingers and slowly made circles around the hardened tips.

He sat up and began to slowly lick small circles all the way around, until he had a mouth full. Her neck fell back as she closed her eyes and let out a long, soft breath expressing her delight. He pulled her back down on top of him and again kissed her ever so long and so passionately. With that, they began making love the rest of the evening and into the morning. Neither one had felt like this in a long, long time. Their first night was magical, and they knew they belonged together.

7

aolo had returned to Carmel to participate in the Concours d'Elegance at Pebble Beach. Victoria had told him about the event during his visit to her in Carmel last October. He loved the idea of competing in a car show in the United States. Right away, he had requested to participate and was accepted. His 1931 Bugatti Royale Victoria Coupe was the one he was flying in that evening. Out of his collection of antique cars, it had to be that one. After all, it had the name Victoria in its title! She was very pleased that he had selected that one. He'd driven her around in it when she was with him in Italy and she'd been bragging to all of her friends about it.

Victoria had been staying with Paolo in a suite at the Pebble Beach Lodge since his arrival. She had wanted to avoid staying at her home during his visit so they could have some privacy. Her daughter Abbey and her new fiancé Armando were there. Abbey owns a real estate company in Monterey called Rite Monterey Realty. She had met her fiancé Armando the previous year during an investigation that had involved one of her listings.

Armando was an agent with the CIA and had been sent to investigate the murder that occurred. It had also involved espionage. They'd fallen in love and became engaged right away. Armando had requested a transfer and was now living with her in the home Victoria and Abbey owned in Carmel.

The suite at the Lodge had a lovely terrace that overlooked the 18th fairway at Pebble Beach, where the car would be displayed. The views of Carmel Beach were spectacular. The white soft sand and the Monterey Cypress trees were majestic. Point Lobos was visible at a distance. While they were enjoying their lunch on the terrace in their white terrycloth robes, Victoria was telling Paolo about all of the festivities they would be attending revolving around the Concours week. There were cocktail parties, dinners, gallery events...

"I can't wait to introduce you to everyone! We're going to meet my friend Catherine at the gallery event. She can't wait to see you again! And I can't wait to see my name sake Darlin', what time does the car arrive?"

"The plane is supposed to be here around 8:00 PM. They're going to keep her in a hanger at the airport until the car trailer comes to take her to the golf course. It will be in there overnight with several other cars until morning. I flew in one of my mechanics to stay with her while she's on display. He's staying in a hotel near the airport. When they come to get the Victoria, he'll stay with her to make sure she's okay, and get her all polished up."

"Oh that's wonderful Sugah', I can't wait to see her. I bought the cutest outfit to wear and it matches her perfectly!" said Victoria. She sounded even more southern when she got excited. "I even bought you a tie the same color so we can be 'matchie-matchie.'"

Paolo loved listening to Victoria talk. She was so full of life and was so bubbly. Her smile was delightful.

"I can't wait to show you off as well, Bella. The cars will pale in comparison to your beauty," he said as he smiled at her and poured more champagne.

Victoria blushed, "Oh Darlin' you say the most romantic things. I just love being with you."

She stood and went to sit on Paolo's lap. She kissed him and he couldn't resist her.

Paolo reached inside the pocket of his bathrobe, pulled out a blue velvet box and put it on Victoria's lap.

"I brought you a little something to wear when we visit her."

Victoria grabbed the box and smiling said, "Darlin', you know I love surprises! What is it? What is it?"

"Open it, see if you like them." Paolo helped Victoria open the beautiful box and exposed a double strand of pearls from Mallorca Spain. "I picked them up for you last time I was there on business and went to see an old friend of mine who owns a jewelry store. He specializes in pearls, and I had him strand these just for you Bella."

"Oh Paolo," she said with a gasp, "they are the most beautiful pearls I've ever seen! Put them on me, Darlin' please."

Victoria dropped her white bathrobe down to her waist, exposing her breasts. She held her hair up in the back. Paolo took the pearls out of the box and placed them on her, softly kissing the back of her neck. "Their beauty doesn't compare to you, my Bella."

"Oh Paolo, they are divine! I can't wait to show Catherine!"

Victoria began to kiss Paolo. He stood, picking her up. Her robe completely fell to the floor. He walked with her into the bedroom and gently laid her on the bed. He dropped his bathrobe as well, so she could see what she had already done to him. He was ready.

"Come here, Sugah,'" she said, wiggling her index finger at him. "Let me show you a proper southern girl thank you."

Paolo melted at her southern drawl and did as he was told. They spent the rest of the afternoon together in delight.

8

Carlota had summoned Gustavo to the gallery at about six that evening. By then, Lindsay had gone home and things had slowed down a bit. There was a lot of foot traffic in front of the store, but mostly it was people going for supper. When he arrived, she led him in the back to the office and closed the door. Her stress level had gone through the roof worrying that Gustavo would screw everything up and she'd be out all the money she had paid for the painting. She was still trying to make the right contact to sell the painting to. She wanted to get rid of it quickly and get her money, but she also had to take her time and make sure it was with the right person.

"Now, tell me again our plan. Tell me what you're going to do," she said, out of breath.

Gustavo shook his head at her and said, "You worry too much. Everything is going to be fine. I'm going to sit in the bar at the airport and watch for the flight to come in. I can see the private planes go to the hangers from up there. I'll watch until everyone has left and I'll get in the hanger and find the car. I know what a Bugatti looks like, I'm not stupid. You gave me the picture anyway. I'll unscrew the steering wheel and get the painting and put it in that tube you gave me and bring it straight here. It'll be fine, don't worry!"

"So help me Gustavo," said Carlota, "if you screw this up I will kill you with my bare hands! We wouldn't be in this mess if you hadn't bankrupted us again. You come straight here, you hear me?"

"Yes yes, I hear you. I'll come straight here with it, you'll see. I won't blunder this, I promise."

His skin crawled at the sound of her voice. He was going to show her he wasn't the pathetic little man she always accused him of being. Gustavo turned and walked out of the gallery.

He hated his sister. She had always been so controlling; he wished her dead. Their mom had died when he was still a kid and she'd taken over his care. Because he hadn't been a normal child, and had special needs due to his scoliosis, she had given herself permission to boss him around. Partly because she had never married, she felt she was the only one who knew what was best for him. He had always drowned his sorrows by drinking and gambling as an adult. He'd take off and go to Las Vegas just to get away from her and have a little fun.

There had been a young Puerto Rican woman who was a maid to a wealthy family in Pebble Beach he'd fallen in love with. They met when he was hired to paint portraits of the family she worked for. A few dinners and some dates later, she had declared her love for him as well. Carlota had put her foot down and had a fit when he shared they had plans to marry. Partly because she would then lose the control over the only person she had to push around. She selfishly paid the woman to move away, robbing him of the only chance at happiness he was ever going to have. He had never forgiven her for that.

At about seven that evening, he arrived at Monterey Airport and went upstairs to the bar and ordered a beer. The large windows allowed you to see the whole tarmac as well as the hangers that housed many private planes. This time of the year, it was always full of Lear jets and other private planes that had arrived for the events. At about 8:15, a large jet touched down and taxied its way toward the private hanger area. After about half an hour of people going in and out, the belly of the plane dropped. Gustavo watched as a golf cart backed up the ramp and inside the plane. Shortly after that, it slowly rolled back, pulling behind it a trailer with a covered vehicle. He watched as they pushed it into one of the hangers.

Gustavo was a bit on edge. He was waiting until he could see no one in the area. He was nervous himself, as he had a plan of his own. He saw this as an opportunity to sell the painting on his own and had planned to double cross his sister. He had hired a man he knew from Las Vegas to steal the painting and was going to meet him the next day for the final plans. But right now, he had to make his move and make sure he wasn't seen.

At about eleven forty-five, there didn't seem to be any movement around the hangers. Two of the guys who had been hanging around had gotten into a truck and driven away.

Thinking they might have just left for a while to get something to eat, Gustavo decided to make his move. He paid his tab and went down the elevator to the main terminal.

As he walked over to the plane hangars, he had to pass through the car rental area. He was glad he was short. It wasn't easy to spot him as he walked around the back of the minivans and he made his way closer. As he approached the hangars, he was careful not to be spotted. He was wearing a Ferrari jacket he owned and a black baseball cap. He figured the jacket would be a deterrent if some-one did actually spot him. He went straight to the hangar he'd seen the car driven to. The front door was open and there were no visible cameras.

Quickly, he walked up and down the rows of vehicles looking for the Bugatti. It was draped with a cover that had a picture of the Italian flag. When he spotted it, his heart really began to race. This was it: now or never.

Gustavo saw that the car cover was only held down with elastic. He lifted it on the driver's side by the door and climbed up onto the front seat behind the steering wheel. It was dark, and he knew he had to work quickly.

Out of his jacket pocket, he took out a pen light, lit it and placed it in his mouth. He took out a screwdriver he had purchased just for this night. It had the multiple heads because he didn't know what size he would need. Good thing, because the first two he tried were not the right size. It was hot under there, and his forehead began to sweat.

His hands were shaking as he tried the different tips on the tool. He finally found one that fit and began to try to twist the screws. It was obvious that the man who removed the steering wheel before had not twisted the screws too tight and he was grateful for that.

He moved quickly and removed the three screws, being careful not to scratch the walnut it was covered in. Carefully, he put them in his shirt pocket.

The steering wheel required a good size tug to get it to lift. It was hard to do with the cover impeding his work space, but he managed to get it off.

Gustavo was sweating profusely now. He took the pen light out of his mouth and shone it inside the steering column. He could see the painting in there wrapped in plastic kitchen wrap. He shook his head at the manner it had been stored. Carefully, he stuck two fingers inside and gently glided it out and placed it on the seat next to him. Quickly he replaced the steering wheel and began to place the screws back. He knew this time, he would have to tighten them much more quickly than when he removed them. He was afraid of running out of time.

When he finished, he took a handkerchief out of his pants pocket and cleaned the steering wheel and column for finger prints, and made sure he looked around on the floor for anything that could have fallen out. He slipped the painting inside his jacket and slipped out from between the door and the cover. The door closed loud, and he panicked, hoping no one was there to hear it.

He scurried out from between the cars, making his way toward the door again, looking around in every direction. He could feel his heart pounding in his throat.

Once he was outside, he tried to walk as if he was in no hurry so as not to attract any attention. Back through the rental car lot he went, in the direction of the short-term parking area.

Once he reached his car, he locked himself in and tried to catch his breath. His hands were still shaking and the sweat poured off of his forehead. He unscrewed the white cardboard tube his sister had given him and slipped the painting inside. Reaching for his phone, he sent her a text that he was on his way.

It was almost one in the morning when he got to the art gallery. Carlota was panicking and pacing when he arrived. She had taken a Xanax to try to calm down. Her doctor had given her a prescription about a month before when she went to see him for her nerves. This whole financial crisis had put her at wits end, and not only was she a nervous wreck, but her blood pressure was sky high.

They went into the back office and carefully took the painting out of the tube. She unrolled it on her desk top and they both looked at it with excitement. It was amazing! The colors were so well preserved it was not going to require any touching up at all.

Gustavo took out his phone and snapped a quick picture.

"We must be careful repacking this. We can't take a chance of ruining it. This is our ticket out of the poor house," said Carlota. "Good job, Gustavo. Now let's go home and get some sleep. I have to be here early tomorrow again."

Carlota was relieved this whole evening was over with and knew she would have no trouble getting some rest. She was exhausted mentally as well as physically.

Gustavo drove home that night knowing he had to meet with his Vegas connection in the morning. As he drove, he finalized his big plan in his head. He knew soon he would be done with Carlotta. That brought a big smile to his face. Now he had to get busy with the finishing touches in his plan, and he didn't have much time.

9

*C*arlota left for the gallery early in the morning. Gustavo had purposely not left his room. He didn't want to have to see his sister. He was afraid she might detect his nervousness and suspect he was up to something.

When he heard the garage door close, he stepped quietly over to the kitchen window and saw her driving away. He was relieved that she was gone. He poured himself a cup of coffee and sat in the kitchen to make his phone call. Nervously, he searched his phone for the number.

He had met Harry "The Shark" Shapiro years ago in Vegas. Harry was often employed by people in and around Vegas to assist with the collection of money owed to some of the not-so-reputable bookies in town. He often sat in on some of the poker games Gustavo frequented when he was there. These were serious games that were off the grid for most of the weekend gamblers just looking for a good time. Harry was a suave-looking fellow who looked to be in his mid-forties. He always dressed sharp and had his hands manicured. The women were always hanging all over him. He was one of these guys who didn't say much about his business, but everyone knew you just didn't mess with him. Even the mob bosses used Harry. He would get the job done, and done professionally. You gave him an assignment, and he did it; no questions asked. Not before, and not after. It just got done and there was never a connection. Heaven knows who he has so graciously assisted in disappearing.

Gustavo had gone drinking one night with Harry, and rambled on about how much he hated his sister. Harry had mentioned to Gustavo that if he ever needed his help for anything, he should give him a call. And so Gustavo did. Not to get rid of his sister, but to help him get his hands on the painting. The theft of the painting alone would probably push Carlota over the edge all by herself, and he wanted to see her suffer for all the suffering she had caused him. He just wanted it to look like a robbery or something, and he didn't want it to implicate him in any way. And Carlota couldn't exactly report the painting missing, so it would be the perfect crime. She would be the only one who knew it was gone, and he would get away with it.

The phone rang, and Harry answered.

"Hey buddy, right on time. I'm here in town. Where do you want to meet? You wanna go get a bite somewhere?

"No!" exclaimed Gustavo. "I can't risk being seen with you anywhere very public. I was thinking the library would be good. I never go in there, so no one will recognize me. I checked it out, and if you go upstairs, there is an area in the back with a couch and some reading chairs. I thought I would meet you up there and give you the cash with an invitation to the gallery party so you can go and mingle. That way you can check out the place and figure out what the easiest way to get in will be. How about 11:30 this morning? You can't miss it. It's right on the corner of Ocean and Lincoln."

"I'm staying right around the corner. I can walk there," said Harry. "I like your little town, Gusty. Looks like a place you can have a good time. What do you want me to do with the goods when I get them?"

Gustavo didn't want to meet up with Harry again and risk being seen together. "Drive by my house and slip it in the mail box. Send me a text and I'll go down and get it.

That way the old bag won't hear anything. Okay?"

"Sounds good. I'll see you at the library later," said Harry.

Later that morning, Gustavo left for his rendezvous with Harry. He walked into the library and was glad not to see anyone at the front desk. He quickly ran up the stairs with a newspaper he had purchased under his arm. When he reached the area in the back, Harry was already seated reading a newspaper. Gustavo sat in the chair adjacent to the one Harry was in. There wasn't another soul in the place. They exchanged pleasantries and Gustavo laid the rolled-up newspaper on the chair between them.

"20K," said Gustavo, "it's all there, and the envelope with the addresses and time for the gallery thing is in there too. And the directions to my place. It's not far."

Harry put his hand over his mouth and leaned his head forward so Gustavo could hear him. He was speaking in a low tone. "Is it in the denominations I requested?"

Gustavo leaned close as well. "Just like you like it. Fifties and hundreds. I'll wait for your text tomorrow night. I'm gonna leave first now, okay?"

Gustavo stood up and walked down the stairs and out the door. He wasn't good at this sort of thing, either. His nerves were on edge too. He had planned all of this in his head, and now it was here and it was happening fast. He knew he was going to have to make the final arrangements to get away very soon. But he had to be very careful about it so she wouldn't suspect anything. He was going to try to avoid her as much as possible so he wouldn't let anything slip. It was a good thing she was so busy with the arrangements for the party to even think about what he was doing. He was just going to lay low and finish his painting projects for now. And wait for that text.

10

Wednesday morning, Victoria and Paolo left her home around 11:00 AM headed to the Seventeen Mile Drive in Pebble Beach. They had visited with her daughter Abbey during breakfast, and agreed to meet up with them later that evening at the gallery party. Armando, Abbey's fiancé, was due back later that afternoon, and they were going to go to have dinner together after they left the party at the gallery. Victoria was driving her BMW with the music blaring when they arrived at the guard gate. He waved them through when he saw the sticker on her car that showed they were guests at the Lodge. They were on their way to see Paolo's car that was on display for the Concours. It should be in place by now, and he wanted to see how it looked and make sure his mechanic had it in good running order, and that the special wax that was supposed to be on the car was in good condition.

The roads wound through the many pines that have been there for generations, and it's maintained in pristine condition. The drive was beautiful. Pebble Beach is home to some of the most expensive and largest mansions on the Monterey Peninsula. The golf courses there are magnificent. Many of the homes belong or have belonged to famous movie stars and rock stars. There are deer that run around on the golf courses and are so used to the golfers they pay no attention to them and they think nothing of interrupting anyone's golf game. Many of the drives along the ocean have sea lions and wild squirrels that sun themselves on the rocks along the ocean. The water is dotted with many sea otters that float effortlessly on their backs near the shore. *There is truly no place on earth more beautiful than the Monterey Peninsula*, Victoria thought.

When they arrived back at the lodge, Paolo got a golf cart and drove it over to where the car was placed on the 18th hole. Many of the real classics were already in place.

Paolo spotted his mechanic right away and made his way to where the car was. Paolo walked over to Victoria's side of the cart and helped her out. They walked over to the car and she was beaming with excitement. She ran up and started to take pictures of it with her cell phone for her sister back in Italy and her Mom in Charleston, South Carolina.

Paolo and the mechanic shook hands and began a conversation in Italian. Victoria understood much of it, but really had no interest in what was going on. She got in the car and wanted Paolo to take her picture, but he continued the conversation. He looked serious, and she assumed there was a problem right away. Stepping out, she made her way to where the two of them were talking.

"Sugah', what's happening? Is everything all right with the car?"

"Bella," he said with a concerned look on his face, "my man says the car was driving strangely. He finally figured out the cable in the steering column was pinched and he can't figure out how it could have happened. He is very concerned that someone has purposely tried to damage her, but he managed to fix the problem. The car has to be in good running condition to be in the display, or I will have to remove the entry."

"Oh no Sugah', is it all right now?" she asked with concern.

"Yes, it seems to be, but since he has spent most of the morning fixing the problem, he is behind on the waxing for the weekend. But he says he will work until it's dark to try to catch up on the lost time. Why don't we go to the Lodge and have some lunch. Aren't we supposed to meet your friend Catherine there now?"

"Why yes, I nearly forgot. I'm so glad you remembered. I can't wait to show her my new pearls! Let's go Sugah'. I have an appointment at the spa later to get ready for tonight's party at the gallery."

As they drove away, Paolo waved at the mechanic, but was still puzzled at the occurrence with his car. How could this have happened? He tried to get it out of his mind so as to enjoy the day, but it continued to bother him.

When they arrived at the Lodge, he requested a table outside. It was such a lovely day. Victoria got a call from Catherine telling her she was pulling up to the valet and she would meet them shortly. She was going to powder her nose first.

When Catherine finally got there, Paolo had already ordered some wine and got up to pull out Catherine's chair. Paolo kissed Catherine in both cheeks, like they do in Europe, and pushed her chair in as she sat down.

"I just love the Mediterranean men. They are so gallant," said Catherine. "I have so much to tell you! You aren't going to believe it!"

"Well Sugah', spill the beans! You look like you are just bustin' at the seams. Tell us! What is it?" inquired Victoria.

"Well, I had an appointment with Madam Manon yesterday afternoon. Paolo, she is a medium I see occasionally for guidance. She lives in Pacific Grove."

"Catherine, you are an intelligent woman, how can you spend your money on such things?" asked Paolo.

"Oh no darlin,'" said Victoria. "She is wonderful! She is always right on the money with what she tell us. If she says something is going to happen, you can take it to the bank. Why she even told me I was going to meet a handsome stranger during my last trip to Italy, and here you are!"

Paolo rolled his eyes and laughingly said, "All right Catherine, tell us your news. This should be very interesting."

"Well," continued Catherine, "Madam Manon says we are going to have a wonderful time during this week, but that it's going to be tainted with death and murder!"

Victoria's mouth dropped open and her eyes got real big. "Murder!" she said as she gulped her wine. "Well, it's a good thing Armando is coming back today. He can protect us with that big scary gun of his!"

"Ladies," laughed Paolo, "there will be no murder. You will see. Now let's just enjoy the day and our lunch. You don't want to be late for the hair appointment later, do you? Now Bella, show Catherine your new pearls."

"Oh Sugah', I almost forgot. But you'll see. What she says will happen, will happen. See Catherine, aren't they lovely?"

11

When Carlota arrived at the gallery, the florist was pulling up at the same time. Just after they went in, the catering company arrived as well. Lindsay was helping set up the bar at the back of the gallery as the flowers were being distributed throughout the different rooms. Carlota was going to have champagne and wine served to the guests. There was to be hors d'ouevres passed around as well. There was a bartender and two servers coming. The gallery had a main room which contained mostly paintings from the local artist and was packed with artwork. There were two other rooms off the main room. The powder room and the office are way in the back. One of the two rooms featured some sculptures and glass art. The other room had mixed varieties of larger paintings placed there by artists from all over. Each of the back rooms had a large upholstered bench the length of the room for people to sit and admire the artwork. Carlota had borrowed a small Picasso from a friend and collector who lives in Pebble Beach and who was going to be in attendance. She placed it at the front window. The florist had made a high style arrangement that had the colors in the painting and he placed them in the window right next to it. Everything was coming together.

Carlotta was a nervous wreck. She went into her office and pulled out the bottle of the Xanax her doctor had given her. As she turned the bottle over to get a pill out, Lindsay walked in to ask a question. She startled Carlotta and the pills spilled all over the floor.

"Didn't your mother teach you to knock before you go into a room?" snapped Carlota.

"The door was open. Here, let me help you," said Lindsay as she got on her knees to help pick up the pills.

"What is it?" Carlota asked in a loud voice.

"The caterer needs to leave. He needs to put the food in the fridge in here. I just wanted to make sure it was okay for him to come in," replied Lindsay as she handed the pills over to her. "You should take it easy on this stuff you know. You could get addicted or something."

"Mind your own business. Send them in here." Carlota stood up and poured the pills back in the bottle. She decided she would take two pills instead of one. She was too much on edge. As she swallowed the pills, the caterer came in with boxes full of several dozen small trays. He placed them into the fridge and told Carlota he needed his check. She was annoyed, but wrote him a check and handed it to him.

"I'll be back to pick up the empty trays tomorrow afternoon. Just put the empty ones right in the box. Don't worry about cleaning them or anything," he said as he left.

Carlota was having second thoughts about leaving the Matisse at the gallery. It was still in the white cardboard tube she and Gustavo had placed it in. She had placed the tube in a basket in her office, next to the filing cabinets. She had other same size tubes in there and it just mixed in. No one would suspect there was anything of any value in there, since all of the other tubes were empty. They are commonly used to mail posters and prints all of the time.

She decided that she would leave it where she had put it. After tomorrow, she'd get to work on securing a buyer. Right now, she had to get through tonight. Everything had to be perfect. After all, she was known as the queen of the gallery events. She told Lindsay she was going to run home and change he clothes real quick so she could come back and relieve her. That way Lindsay could go and get dressed, too. She locked the office door behind her and drove off, feeling a bit more relaxed now that everything was ready for tonight's event.

When she got home, Gustavo was in his gallery in the back of the house working on a painting. There were opened tubes of oil paint everywhere. There were canvases stacked on the floor. The place was always a mess, but artists aren't known for their neatness. He was facing the door and she couldn't see what he was working on, nor could she care less. She had enough to worry about now. She was just glad he was busy and out of her hair.

The hot lights were clipped on the easel that was facing the window, to dry the oil on the painting he had just finished. He was trying to hide his nerves when she stuck her head in to tell him she had only come home to change.

"I won't be home until late. You'll have to figure out dinner for yourself," she said.

"Good luck tonight," said Gustavo as he heard her walk toward the garage door. He hadn't even wanted to make eye contact with her.

His brush shook in his hand. When she left the room, he had to stop and sit in a chair and take deep breaths. It was too late to stop what he had already started; and he didn't really want to either. Now he had to plan his getaway. But it was too soon. He had to pick the right time.

Gustavo smiled at the thought of his sister's misery when she discovers the painting she had planned to sell was gone. He pictured her screaming and crying at the thought of her ruin. *Maybe she'll even commit suicide!* he thought to himself. He laughed out loud and went back to his painting. Time was running out, and things had to look as normal as possible. He couldn't give even one hint of anything being out of place. Besides, painting always relaxed him.

12

It was about four in the afternoon and Carlota opened the door to the gallery. The soft jazzy music was playing in the background. The food was all set. The wait staff was in place. Lindsay looked fabulous in her black designer cocktail dress that accentuated her double D's, and Carlotta looked nice and matronly. That was about as good as she could get in her black suit, and after all, she had legs with cankles, and orthopedic shoes. She was sporting a diamond broach she had purchased the year before. It was the only fancy thing she could muster up.

She was nervous and began to pace up and down.

"Lindsay, go stand in the door way so people can see you as they go by."

Lindsay did as she was told. She stood there and waved at the cars going down Ocean Avenue. At about four twenty, the first group of people showed up. Carlotta greeted them at the door and waved the wait staff over with a tray of champagne and hors d'ouevres. The small chit chat was taking place as more guests arrived. Lindsay turned on the charm and before you knew it, the place was packed. Cars were driving up and down the street, looking for a parking spot. Most people went to park at the public parking lot one block up.

At five, Victoria, Paolo, and Catherine showed up.

"Hello Sugah,'" Victoria said as she walked over to Carlota to give each other a kiss on the cheek.

"This is my Paolo, you know, the handsome Italian I told you about when we last spoke. He has a car entered in the Concours. You'll simply have to come up to see it

this weekend. You *must* get away and come by. It's a fabulous Bugatti convertible called The Victoria of course."

"It's lovely to meet you Paolo," said Carlota as she extended her hand. "I'll do my best to get by to see it. As you can see this is a very busy time for me, but I will try. Hello Catherine, so good of you to come," she said as she gave Catherine a hug.

"Carlota, this is a fabulous event! Why, I think there is even more people here than last year," she said as she grabbed a glass of champagne from the waiter. "Oh, look Victoria, I think I see Abbey and Armando at the door. I'll go and get them. Excuse me Carlota. We'll have to do lunch soon. Thanks for having us," she said as she walked toward the entrance to retrieve the couple.

Abbey and Armando walked over toward Victoria and Paolo. Catherine walked toward some people she knew to greet them. It was definitely a social gathering for the locals, mixed in with the attending celebrities. The sound in the room got louder, and the place got packed. Everyone was happy and the sales began to take place.

There were television actors, politicians, movie stars, golfers, well-known business CEOs, to name a few, and they were all buying!

Carlota was beaming. Lindsay was walking around flirting at the un-escorted men and passing out champagne. Carlota was greeting all of her guests and swiping credit cards left and right.

The newspaper reporters were there, snapping pictures of everyone coming and going. The local TV station was outside trying to catch an interview with anyone who would stop. Everything was going as planned.

Just a couple of blocks away, Harry Shapiro had checked out of his room and was taking care of his bill in cash. Earlier that morning, he had moved his car to the public parking lot a block from the art gallery. It was an easy walk to anywhere in downtown Carmel and he had spent the day just strolling up and down Ocean Avenue. Returning to his room about three, he had showered and slipped into his black Armani suit with a red silk shirt. He looked in the mirror and waved his hand over his jet black hair, smoothing it straight back. Then, he squirted his favorite cologne on to his matching red silk pocket handkerchief and placed it in his top jacket pocket. Harry was always immaculately dressed. He had a very savoir faire look about him. His nails were always manicured. His hair was always quaffed perfectly. His suits and shoes were always designer. He wore a gold pinky ring on his left hand along with his Rolex and a gold bracelet on his right hand. He finished putting items in his pants and jacket pockets. He had a pair of black gloves he slipped into the inside pocket of his jacket, along with a small, leather pencil-like pouch. In his front pants pocket, he placed his bulging money clip, and his Swiss knife. One last look and he was ready. It was four-thirty and he zipped up his small bag and walked into the bathroom. He took a wash cloth and made it damp. He carefully wiped down the entire room for any fingerprints, including the TV clicker. He took the elevator to the lobby. He walked up to the desk and placed his room key and a twenty on the counter. The older man on duty was on the phone, and just gave him a wave as he saw him turn and walk away, without really looking up.

Harry walked the two short blocks to the parking lot near the gallery and placed his bag inside the trunk. He turned in the direction of the gallery and made his way toward it. He was surprised the place was so full of people, but glad at the same time. The more people, the less he would be noticed. Making his way inside, he began to look around. As he walked, he noticed Lindsay with a tray of champagne flutes. Her eyes caught his and she made her way to where he stood. She thought he seemed like a man that would be loaded. Just her kind of man!

"Care for some champagne?" she asked as she smiled and bobbed her head from left to right.

"Thank you sweetheart," he said as he winked at her. Don't you look lovely this evening? Do you work here?" he asked as he sipped from the flute.

"Yes, I work here part time. But it's only temporary," she said as she took a deep breath and rolled her shoulders back, raising her boobs in his direction. "I'm just saving my money until I can get to L.A. and get a modeling contract or get an acting job. I want to be a hostess on a game show. They get to wear all kinds of cool clothes and travel and stuff."

"I can see that," he said, as he checked her out from top to bottom. "I know people down there, you know?" he said. Her eyes lit up and she smiled bigger.

"This one is one fry short of a Happy Meal," he thought. "What time do you get off, sweetheart?" he asked as he winked again. "Perhaps we can get a drink after the event and we can talk about your big move?"

"Oh I'd really like that!" exclaimed Lindsay. "Everyone should be gone by around eight. They all go to dinner and Carlota will close and go home. Her feet'll be killing her by then. She'll be too tired to stay here after and won't need me until tomorrow to clean up."

"Magnificent!" he said. "Where can we meet?"

She thought for a moment and said, "There is a place around the corner that used to belong to the ex-mayor. You know the actor that was the mayor here. It's called the Hog's Breath. We can meet there right after I'm done. Are you going to hang out here for a while? I have to circulate, you understand?"

"Sure, sure, I understand. I'll just take a look around and we'll meet there later. Don't worry, I'll just sit at the bar and look forward to meeting up with you later. We'll discuss your big move to L.A..."

"Cool! Talk to you later."

Harry watched as she shook her bottom when she turned and walked away. He certainly enjoyed looking at her.

"This is going to be fun," he thought to himself as he began to walk around. All of the guests were all talking to someone. Once in a while, there was the occasional glance in his direction, but he tried to make as little eye contact as possible. He sipped his champagne and walked around the gallery, pretending to look at the art. All the while, he was casing the place, trying to figure out how to get back in. In case he didn't have a clear passage, he now had plan B.

Walking around from one room to another, he noticed the windows were really just stained glass that didn't really open. They were obviously placed there just to let the light in, not for ventilation. Carmel never really got hot enough, so the air from the front door was all that was needed. As he walked toward the rear, he noticed the bathrooms, the back service door, and a door that was marked 'Office." It was ajar, and he pushed it slightly to look inside. He noticed a desk against the far wall, and on the floor next to it, a large basket stuffed with white cardboard mailing tubes.

"Bingo," he thought to himself. That's my target. Easy Breezy. That's what he'd be after later.

After he'd seen all he needed to see, he made his way to the front. He made eye contact with Lindsay as he walked through. She was near the front door passing out champagne to people entering. He walked up to her and said, "By the way, sweetheart, what's your name?"

"Oh yeah, huh?" she said as she giggled. "It's Lindsay."

"I'm Harry. See you in a bit." He leaned over to give her a kiss on the cheek and slid his mouth down to the crook of her neck and gave her a little bite.

Lindsay got turned on right away. It didn't take much for her, though. She had always been on the horny side. In high school, she couldn't figure out what the big deal all the other girls were always talking about waiting for. Waiting for what? She liked getting laid and she did quite often. She lost her virginity during her sophomore year to one of her brother's friends after a basketball game in his car, parked at the Carmel High School parking lot. After that, it was anyone, anytime. She liked sex and was going to get it whenever she could. Now, she had taken a liking to older men. Especially married men. She got off on the fact that they enjoyed her body now that their wives rarely paid any attention to them. She had even gotten one of her regular hook-up guys to pay for her boob job. Most of her regular lovers had money and would meet her at nice hotels and buy her clothes and give her cash. That was her thing, and she was going to use her body to get everything she wanted.

Harry was looking forward to meeting up with her later. But he thought it was a shame she'd be the sacrifice to his plan. He too was used to getting what he wanted at any expense. He had a job to do, and he would get it done without a second thought to anyone's sacrifice. He was to retrieve that painting and that was his focus. He disappeared around the corner and walked down the street to the place where they were going to rendezvous.

13

As the evening continued, everyone began to disburse. It was dinner time, and most all the guests had some place else to go. Some were attending other parties or going out for a nice dinner.

Carlota stood at the door, shaking hands with everyone and thanking them for coming.

Earlier that evening at around six-thirty, Victoria had suggested they all go out to eat around the corner, and they had said their goodbyes to Carlota. They had all gone to the Hogs Breath for convenience. They had all taken different vehicles, and that was one place close they could all walk to. Besides, it was a nice evening.

They had all wanted to take the time to catch up with Armando and Abbey. Armando had been away for a couple of weeks. His CIA work would sometimes take him out of state. His territory was most of the west coast. And this was the start of the busy season for Abbey's real estate office, Rite Monterey Realty. The office was busy preparing for all of the out-of-town buyers who would hit the Peninsula with their fat wallets. Everyone who visits here this time of the year falls in love with the area, and many end up buying vacation homes or condos.

They made a lovely couple and had fallen in love the previous year. Armando Shear was a gorgeous tall man with brown hair, and a smile to die for. He had a great dimple.

Abbey was a beautiful blonde with eyes you could swim in. She was her mother's only child. Abbey had Victoria's Southern beauty and charm. Armando met Abbey the previous year when he'd been sent to the Peninsula for a murder that had taken place in one of Abbey's listings. The chemistry was amazing, and Armando put in for a transfer to the Peninsula so they could be together. He moved in with Abbey while they made plans for the future. Victoria wasn't home much, so she approved of the situation. She was always traveling and didn't spend much time in the house.

As they got up to leave the restaurant, Armando made his way to the door first to hold it open for the ladies. As he swung it open, Lindsay came running in.

"Oh thanks," she said as she ran in toward the bar. Armando looked in the direction she was headed as everyone exited. He noticed a man seated at the bar with his back to the door. Lindsay made her way to where he was seated. As she made walked toward him, Armando stepped outside and closed the door. But something made the hair in the back of his neck stand. He always had a sense for trouble. His extensive training was part of it. But he decided not to give it a second thought. This wasn't his business. Tonight was all about him and Abbey spending quality time together. And they had been enjoying everyone else's company.

Once outside, they said their goodbyes and went their separate ways. Abbey couldn't wait to get Armando home, and Paolo and Victoria drove Catherine to her house before returning to the Lodge.

"Hey, sorry I'm late," said Lindsay as she pulled the stool out next to Harry.

"No worries sweetheart, what can I get you?" Harry had planned on getting her wasted so he could better use her for his plan. He needed a way back into the gallery, and she was going to have to be it.

"What are you having?" she asked with a giggle.

"Scotch and soda, you want one?"

"Sure, I like Scotch. Make it a double, I've had a busy night and I need to unwind."

Harry waved at the bartender and ordered two double Scotch and sodas. As he waited for them to arrive, he began to run his fingers through Lindsay's hair and massaged the back of her neck. She smiled at him and she wanted him to know she liked it.

No sooner had the bartender put the drinks down Lindsay picked hers up and downed it.

"Wow," said Harry, "You must be stressed. Here, have mine," and he slipped his drink it in front of her. He continued to massage the back of her neck.

"Thanks," she said, giggling. "I've had a busy night. That witch has been working me like crazy. I only get ten dollars an hour and she has me doing everything for her. And she's raking in the dough tonight, too. You'd think she'd give me a bonus or something, but all she gave me was this dress. It's cool though, you like my dress?"

"Well, what there is of it! Yes it looks really nice on you. It accentuates your...best features." Harry slipped his hand down her bare back, softly caressing it. He knew this was going to be easy.

"So, you want to be a model?" he asked as he watched her down the second Scotch and soda. He waved at the bartender and told him to keep them coming.

Lindsay began telling Harry all about her big plans to move to Hollywood and be a model for a game show. He watched as she continued to drink. She told him she wanted to get on "Price is Right" or maybe replace Vanna White someday. She went on and on about her big plans and he kept getting her liquored up.

It didn't take long before Lindsay began reacting to Harry's touch. She liked his soft caress, and she started to get turned on. She reached under the bar and grabbed his crotch. Now Harry knew he was getting close.

"You feel nice," she said as she felt him grow at her touch. "How old are you anyway?" she asked. "You feel pretty good for someone older. I like older men; did I tell you I like older men?" Now she was definitely wasted.

Lindsay had begun slurring her words. Harry knew he had to make his move pretty soon, or she wouldn't be able to walk. He began kissing her. She kissed him back and began wanting to pull him out of his pants under the bar.

"I have a great idea," said Harry, "why don't we go someplace where we can be alone? You're really turning me on. Let's get out of here."

"Sounds like a plan," slurred Lindsay, slamming her empty glass on the bar.

Harry pulled a couple of hundred dollar bills and put them on the bar. He reached in his jacket pocket and put on his black gloves. Then he helped Lindsay stand. He put his arm around her as they walked out the door.

"I have an idea," he said. "Why don't we go around the corner to the gallery? I don't think I can wait too long to

be with you. Besides, everyone should be gone by now and we can be together in the same place we met."

"Oh...that's really *romantic*," she slurred. "I have my key right here!" she said as she swung her clutch bag in the air.

Harry looked at his watch. It was eleven o'clock. By now, the street was pretty near empty. People were leaving the restaurants to go home, or had already left to attend other venues. As they walked around the corner, Lindsay was having trouble staying in her stilettos. He bent over and took them off of her so she could walk easier.

"You are such a gentleman," she slurred as they neared the gallery.

When they reached the front door, Lindsay was having trouble getting the key out of her purse. Harry took it out and placed the key in the keyhole and opened the door. He then put the key in his pants pocket.

"Is there an alarm?" he asked.

"Hell no! Carlota is too damn cheap for an alarm. Besides, nothing ever happens in this stinkin' town."

Once inside, Harry told her not to turn on any lights.

"We don't want anyone to disturb us, besides; it's more romantic this way."

Harry asked Lindsay about the small painting in the window. His eye had caught it when he was at the gallery earlier.

"It's just an old Picasso 'cheapo' borrowed from a friend for the party. It goes back tomorrow," she said as she made her way to the back of the gallery. "Come on back here. No one will see us back here. I've always wanted to get laid on one of those fancy benches. Wouldn't she just die if she knew I did it in here?"

Harry watched as Lindsay made her way to the gallery room on the right, in the back. It was the larger of the two rooms. There were two long wide upholstered benches right down the center.

Lindsay reached behind her neck and unhooked the top of her halter dress, exposing her breasts.

"Come and get these babies daddy," she said as she walked over to him. She began kissing him. She knelt down, opened his zipper and pulled him out. Her tongue was all over him. He really was enjoying every minute, but at the same time, he was trying to figure out how he was going to get into the office to steal the Matisse without any witnesses. He stood her up and began kissing her neck. His hands were all over her breasts, and then he began kissing and sucking on them. Lindsay began rubbing herself all over him. He sat on one of the benches and she startled him. She started rotating her hips and they continued making out. He really was enjoying himself. He was big, and could barely control his urges, but knew he couldn't leave any evidence. "You want me to blow you?" she asked. "I'm really good at it. Let me blow you, daddy."

"*Perfect,*" he thought. He had to do away with her, but didn't want to leave any marks. So this was a perfect way to be rid of her so he could get his job done and get the hell out of there.

"Yeah baby, blow me. But let's be safe," he said. He reached into his jacket pocket and pulled out that small leather pouch. He unzipped it and pulled out a rubber. He was having trouble tearing open the packaging with his gloves.

"Aren't you going to take off your gloves?" she asked.

"No, my hands are rough and I don't want to scratch your pretty soft skin," he replied.

"Here, let me help you daddy."

Lindsay peeled open the rubber and helped him slip it on. "You're pretty long aren't you?" she giggled.

"Thanks baby," he said. "Here, I'll give you something extra to make you feel good."

Harry pulled out a small vial with white powder. He began to sprinkle it on himself while she watched.

"Oh, is that Coke?" she asked. "I've always wanted to do it with Coke. I hear it's a real turn on this way. I've snorted it before, but I've never ate it before."

"Well baby, you suck on this and you'll be in heaven in no time," he said with a laugh.

Lindsay knelt on the floor in front of him and began to work on Harry. He held her head down. She was actually pretty good at it and he was really having a good time, when she suddenly began to slow down.

"I feel really funny," she stopped and said.

"Here honey, why don't you lie down on the bench for a minute? It'll pass real soon." Harry knew it wouldn't be long before she was history.

Lindsay got up and laid on the bench. She began convulsing a bit and passed out. Harry watched as she shivered from the seizure like movements as he pulled off the rubber and put it inside a baggie he pulled out of his small leather pouch. He also placed the vial inside and tightly closed it back up. He zipped his pants up. Then he put the leather pouch back inside his jacket pocket. Harry knew she would be taking her last breath soon enough, and didn't want to wait around. He had to get out and get a start toward Vegas before she was found in the morning. It was already after midnight and time was ticking.

He looked inside his pants pocket and pulled out the key. He put the key in the key hole to the office; he quickly opened the door and closed it behind him. There were no windows in the small room, so he turned on the light. Next to the desk, he saw the basket full of the white mailing tubes Gustavo had told him about. He looked for the one that had been marked with a small black ink dot Gustavo had put on the lid. It was barely visible, but he found it without any trouble.

As he walked out of the office, he stuck his head back in the room where Lindsay was. He walked over to her and she was gone. There were no more breath sounds, her mouth was still open and her eyes were shut.

"Really a shame," he thought to himself. *"She really was hot!"*

Harry made his way to the front door and could see from the front window, that the street was empty and no one around. There were no passing cars. He was just about to leave, when his eye caught that Picasso again.

"What the heck," he thought, *"might be worth a few bucks."* He grabbed the Picasso from the front window and he slipped off his jacket, draping it over his left arm to hide the tube with the Matisse and the small Picasso painting. Now all he had to do was dive by Gustavo's house, put the tube in the mailbox, and take his cash home. It was a long drive, but he had a nice big Cohiba he had purchased and was planning on enjoying on the trip home.

14

"You have arrived at your destination," said the voice on Harry's GPS as he slowly pulled up in front of Gustavo and Carlota's Carmel cottage. There were no street lights, and since there weren't numbers in front of the houses, he was glad he had thought to use it or he would have never found the place. Harry put the white tube inside the mailbox and quietly drove back up to Ocean Avenue where he pulled the car over to send the text.

"I got a little surprise for you in the mailbox. I had a blast. Enjoy your life," said the text he sent.

Carlota had returned home around nine that evening, physically and emotionally exhausted from the event and the preceding week. She had found Gustavo in his art room. The first thing she did was go to the kitchen, get a bottle of Brandy out of the cupboard and pour a big tall glass.

"Well, it was a good sale, not that you care," she said with disgust at her brother. "Don't stay up late. You have to come in the morning and help me clean up the place." She turned and went upstairs to drink herself to sleep.

Gustavo finished what he was doing and went upstairs to wait for the text message. He had the television on low, as to not deviate from any of his usual routine. He would usually watch the news at eleven, and then part of one of the late night shows. He always had trouble going to sleep. Tonight, he wouldn't be watching his TV. He would just be watching his cell phone for that text from Harry.

As soon as he read it, he crept out of his room into the hall. He could hear Carlota snoring, so he felt it was safe to go out and get the tube from the mailbox.

He hurried down the stairs and snuck out the back door praying not to clumsily trip over anything that would make noise and wake his sister up. It was dark and cold. The light fog had begun to creep down the street, as is typical in Carmel. Once he reached mailbox, he made sure there wasn't anyone walking a dog who might see him out that late. When he saw the coast was clear, he ran over and retrieved it, then quietly hurried back into the house and upstairs to his room. His heart was pounding out of his chest.

Once inside his room, he closed his door and put the tube on his bed. He twisted it open and slightly pulled the lid off, just far enough to see that the painting was inside.

He didn't dare pull it out. If she woke up and caught him with it in his room, he knew shit would hit the fan. He pushed the lid closed again and hid it in the back of his closet, behind his suitcase. She never looked through his stuff. She was always telling him the place smelled like a horse stall.

He had pulled it off. The painting was now his. His life and future was now his to plan and live as he saw fit.

Gustavo decided to write a letter before going to bed. He would mail it in the morning on his way into the gallery. He had to put the rest of his plan into action before he ran out of time.

When Harry reached the Bixby Bridge on his way down the coast, he opened his window and threw the cheap burner telephone over the rail and into the deep water. No one would ever find it, and there would be no record of the owner of the number should anyone ever have the need to look at Gustavo's call record. It was untraceable. He lit his Cohiba and turned on his CD player to a Spyro Gyra album. It was his favorite jazz driving music. He smiled and almost laughed out loud knowing he had left more of a mess than Gustavo had bargained for. But at the same time, he had left him more of a gift than he had bargained for, too.

15

Gustavo was jolted awake by a loud banging on his bedroom door.

"Get up! We have work to do at the gallery. Where's the Alka Seltzer? I have an awful headache"

Gustavo knew it wasn't a headache. It was a hangover mixed with the Xanax pills Carlota had been taking. He had gone to bed after one in the morning, but had slept like a baby.

After he walked downstairs, he saw Carlota downing a cup of black coffee.

"I didn't have time to make a fresh pot. This is yesterday's. I just put some in the micro. If you want some, you'll have to make it or go to the bakery and buy it. I have to get in there and get those checks deposited and pay some bills right away. The landlord is going to be there in the afternoon. Don't be late! I need you to clean up and go to the bank later." With that, Carlota went out the door to the garage and left in a hurry. Gustavo smiled knowing it was just a matter of time before he never had to listen to her boss him around again.

When Carlota got downtown, she walked fast toward the front door. She had a list of things she needed to take care of. She also had an early afternoon appointment with a musician who attended the event the previous evening. He was coming back to talk with her about purchasing several sculptures.

She parked her car up the street from the gallery. There were plenty of spaces available because it was still early. She walked quickly to the front door, and when she got there, she stopped dead in her tracks: The Picasso wasn't in the window! She went into a panic!

Quickly she opened the door and looked on the floor to see if it had perhaps fallen off the easel, but it wasn't there. Panicking, her heart began to race. She began to sweat profusely.

"Oh no, oh no, oh no..." she repeated over and over. She didn't know where to turn first, or what to do. She ran toward her office door to open it and make sure the Matisse was still in its place, but on her way to the back she sensed something else was wrong. She didn't know why, but she was drawn to the room across from her office.

She tried her office door, but it was still locked. So she walked slowly toward the large room. She switched on the light and there lying on the bench was Lindsay!

Grey in the face, with her breasts exposed and all over her chest!. She had clear foam around her lips. Her arms and legs were spread out and touching the floor.

Carlota was in such shock, she ran screaming out of the gallery onto Ocean Avenue. She stood on the sidewalk making blood-curdling screams and holding her chest. She was about to faint when the pharmacist ran out from the store next to the gallery. She pointed at the door and blacked out.

When she came to, the paramedics were there giving her oxygen and checking her vital signs. She was still on the sidewalk. Bob, the owner of the pharmacy next door was talking to the police.

The paramedics wanted to take Carlota to the hospital, but she wouldn't have it. They helped her up off the sidewalk and gave her a hand walking inside. By now, the place was crawling with the fire department and the police. All the shop owners and employees were standing outside on the sidewalk trying to get a whiff as to what was going on. There was a police officer diverting traffic.

Police Chief Mike Cunningham got a chair for Carlota and helped her sit down. He was at a loss as to what to say first to her. She was hysterical. Someone handed her glass of water.

Chief Cunningham had stopped by the gallery the night before after work, just to make an appearance. He liked attending the events in his city mainly to keep in touch with the citizens of his town. He hadn't seen anything out of the ordinary while he was there. Mike

Cunningham was an attractive man in his middle fifties, with a head full of silver hair. His wife and he had parted ways many years before. He was always available for a game of tennis. That's how he kept in shape. He was strong for a man of his age, and liked jogging on the beach when he could. His favorite doubles partner was Victoria's friend Catherine. They'd been known to hook up once in a while when they felt the need for companionship. He was charming all right, but she always preferred the younger men. So she kept Mike at an arm's length.

"Carlota, that was quite a nice party you had last night," He said as he tried to break the ice and ease into the conversation.

Carlota could see flashes coming from the back of the gallery where Lindsay was. They were taking pictures of the body and the crime scene. The coroner had arrived and was doing his examination before they removed the body. The police had the yellow tape all over the outside and blocked the sidewalk so no one could get near. The gurney had been brought in to remove the body and was sitting in the gallery.

"Did you know Lindsay was coming back here with anyone, or did you see her leave with anyone last night? Was there anything unusual about her behavior that you can tell me?"

"No," said Carlota between whimpers. "I told her to come in early this morning to help clean up as she left. She was just mingling with everyone last night like she was supposed to. But I was busy and didn't see anything out of the ordinary."

"Is there anything else missing other than the painting in the front? Bob says there was a Picasso that's gone. Do you know anything about that? Did you return it to the owner after the party?"

Suddenly, there was a panic that left Carlota weak in the knees. She hadn't even gone into her office to see if the Matisse was still in place.

Gustavo left home for the gallery about half an hour after Carlota. He had no clue as to what was going on there. He drove over to the Carmel Post Office to mail that letter he had stayed up to write before heading in.

When he tried to get down Ocean Avenue toward town, traffic was backed up. It looked like it was going to be a while, so he decided to take some side streets and get there faster.

When he got downtown, he saw that Ocean Avenue was closed off. There was a cop in the middle of the street diverting the traffic. He decided to park two blocks up and walk down.

When he got to the corner of the gallery, he saw the yellow tape everywhere. People were congregating outside on the sidewalk. Fire trucks and police were crawling all over.

Gustavo's heart began to pound a little in his chest. He was worried that Carlota had been stupid and called the police if she had discovered Matisse missing, not thinking that the painting was probably a black market painting. But it seemed unlikely that she would be that stupid. He could feel his heart in his throat, and he could hardly breathe. He was worried that he would be accused of stealing it, or having had something to do with it.

Still unaware of what had happened to Lindsay, he let himself in the back door and quickly opened the office. He was standing by the basket next to Carlota's desk, by the white mailing tubes when she ran in the door with Captain Cunningham behind her.

"Did you see what they did? Oh Gustavo, did you see what they did? They took the Picasso and killed Lindsay!"

Gustavo went pale. His legs went weak. He couldn't believe what she had just said!

"They killed Lindsay? Who killed Lindsay? What do you mean?" He began to sweat and his lips began quiver. He panicked knowing he had hired Harry to steal the painting and was now worried that he'd also killed her. That wasn't what he had in mind. He would have never done anything to hurt anyone. And stealing the Picasso wasn't part of the deal either. He should have known that those kinds of people would do anything to get the job done. And now he was going to have to live with the guilt. The worst part was that he wouldn't be able to tell anyone, or he would be considered an accomplice.

"Mr. Dominguez, you look like you need to sit down," said Captain Cunningham as he walked over and slid a chair under Gustavo.

"I think I'm going to be sick," said Gustavo, looking around for the trash can.

"I need to ask you some questions," said Captain Cunningham. "Do you mind if we just take care of this now?"

Gustavo nodded his head yes as he took some tissue off the desk and used it to wipe his forehead.

"Were you here last night, Mr. Dominguez?"

"No, I was at home. I don't usually attend these things. I'm not very good socially."

Captain Cunningham continued with the questioning.

"Do you know anything or anyone who would want to harm Lindsay, or do you know anything about the Picasso that is missing?"

"No. I hardly knew Lindsay. She just worked for Carlotta part time once in a while. I saw her in passing, but my work keeps me out of here most of the time. I teach at the college and do portraits on the side. I've been busy trying to finish a project," said Gustavo as the spit began to fly from between his two front teeth. It was a very unpleasant side affect from his nerves.

Gustavo looked up at Carlotta as if he expected her to intervene on his behalf.

"My brother was home when I left in the afternoon to come here, and he was home last night when I got there," she offered.

Captain Cunningham ran his fingers through his thick silver hair.

"I'm sorry, but you understand I have to ask these questions. I know you are both very upset. I think you should both go home. We won't be done here for quite a while. There is no sense in your staying. I'm going to have to get the FBI involved. I suspect Lindsay was killed by the thief or thieves for that Picasso. Whenever valuable art is involved, I need to call them in. It's not just a murder investigation now, you know? I'll have one of my officers drive you both home. I'll call you later this evening. Meanwhile, I'll need the name of the owner of the painting. I'll have to go and have a conversation with him as well. You might want to give your insurance a call. I don't know how they are going to want to handle this."

Carlota panicked at the thought of the missing painting. She hadn't been able to pay the insurance premiums for the gallery. She began to hyperventilate. She hadn't told her brother this. Now she felt like she was really ruined. What was she to do? The only ace in her pocket was the Matisse. The money from that, might cover the Picasso, or at least part of it. Soon everyone would know she was broke. The sales from this week would certainly help. But she hadn't had time to count the money yet, and she didn't know just where she stood with that. If she was lucky, she might break even. All these thoughts ran through her head at the same time. It was too much for her to handle.

When the police car pulled up in front of their home, they both got out in silence. Carlota went straight to the cabinet, got a bottle of vodka and ran upstairs. She popped her pill bottle and swallowed more of her pills with as much of the vodka as she could gulp down fast.

Gustavo stood in his gallery, sobbing with his head in his hands. What had he done? *That poor girl.* What had he done?

16

Victoria and Paolo were in their suite at the Lodge early in the morning getting ready to go to the 18th Fairway at Pebble Beach, to hang out with the car and visit with the folks who were passing by and admiring it when her cell phone rang.

"Turn on the TV! Victoria, turn on the TV!" she heard Catherine screaming on the other end.

"Who is it my darling?" asked Paolo, shrugging his shoulders.

"It's Catherine actin' all crazy on the phone line. She's screamin' about turning on the TV. Would you be a dear and turn it on so we can see what she's fussin' all about?"

"You aren't going to believe it, you just aren't going to believe it!" yelled Catherine.

The television went on, and it was set on the local news channel. There was the news woman reporting from downtown Carmel. She was standing in front of Carlota's gallery.

"It is still not known if the Picasso was the only thing taken from the gallery, and how or why Lindsay Reed was murdered. We'll continue bringing you this story as it unravels. Back to you at the station…"

"Jesus take the wheel!" exclaimed Victoria as she threw her hands up and dropped into a chair.

"Bella, I don't understand what that means about the wheel," said Paolo with a puzzled look on his face. But she was always coming up with Southern sayings that made him smile. That was part of her charm.

"Catherine, darlin', come pick me up," said Victoria as she turned to Paolo and said, "I told you, when Madam Manon tells you there's going to be a murder, Sugah' there is going to be a murder! Darlin' you go on today without me. I'm going to have Catherine take me home. I feel the need to bake one of my Peach Pies. It always relaxes me when I bake. It's like therapy. And besides, I simply must go tell Abbey and Armando what's happened."

"I will miss you at my side today, Bella. But I understand. Call me later and I will pick you up." Victoria loved Paolo's Italian accent. She walked over to him and ran her fingers through his hair. She gave him a quick kiss.

"Thank you, Sugah,'" she said softly in his ear. "But don't you fret now. I'll have Catherine visit with me while I bake and she can drive me back to the Lodge. We'll catch up later. Ciao Paolo."

17

Armando and Abbey had spent the night together catching up with their love making. Spending time away from one another when Armando left town for an investigation left them longing for one another immensely. Their chemistry had always been amazing. Armando woke up to the sound of the shower running. He knew Abbey was in there and he wasn't quite through with her yet.

He threw his covers off, and walked over to the shower door. He watched her for a minute as she washed herself with her lufa, slowly moving it up and down her breasts. It only took a second to get him back into attention. He opened the door and stepped inside.

"Good morning, mi Amor. Can I give you a hand?" he said as he tenderly gave her a slow, lingering kiss.

"Mmmmm yes. You can give me both hands if you wish," she said as she kissed him back.

Armando began to move his hands down Abbey's back toward her rear. He cupped it and pressed her closer to him. Abbey began to run her lufa up and down Armando's back as they continued to kiss. She felt him between them, hard and determined. Armando began to lick Abbey's neck and massage her hair. It was covered with that shampoo she used that smelled of gardenias.

The aroma had always made him crazy. He loved her scent. He ran his fingers up into her scalp and began massaging it, making the smell even more intense.

Armando turned Abbey with her back to his hairy chest. She loved the feeling of his soft, velvety chest hairs on her skin. His hands now moved slowly toward her soapy breasts and slowly moved them in circles while he rubbed up against her rear. He began to pinch her nipples and she became even more aroused. Abbey pushed herself back further onto him, and was delighted at his readiness.

She throbbed with eagerness as she could feel him practically inside her.

Armando slipped his soapy hands downward toward her spot. She loved it when he played with it. He slipped two fingers inside of her. She was wet and ready for him. Armando sat on the shower bench and pulled her down on to him. He entered her as she sat down, and continued to play with her spot, making her even more aroused. Abbey went crazy when he teased her as he began to rock her up and down with his hips. Then, he slid his hands on her hips and began to drive her up and down onto him, while he kissed the back of her neck. The sensation of the movement made Abbey lose control. Armando was a master at satisfying her. She had never had a more engaging lover. As the pleasure became more intense, Abbey turned her face to meet Armando's kisses. They were always soft but passionate. They moved faster and deeper with each thrust until the pleasure overtook them and they gave into the moment, exploding with satisfaction. Armando continued to kiss Abbey, caressing her face and her breasts until they both came down from their overpowering moment of bliss. They finished helping one another shower and began to ready themselves for the day. They were both heading to work.

When Catherine and Victoria arrived at her Carmel house with a bag full of peaches and pie baking stuff, she shouted up at the bottom of the stairs.

"Y'all come down here! I have news you won't believe! And Armando, you cover that thing up before you come down here. I don't want to see that thing again!"

Victoria was referring to the first time she met Armando. She had arrived home late from a trip to Italy, and heard Abbey upstairs obviously entertaining. So she had retired to her bedroom to take a short rest until morning. When she awoke, she heard a noise in the kitchen. She threw on her dressing gown and entered only to find Armando at the sink, helping himself to a glass of water, butt naked. The surprised had just about killed him, but the delight at seeing a young man naked at the sink was just what Victoria needed to always tease him about the moment they first met.

Abbey was the first one to arrive downstairs at the kitchen and greeted her mother with a kiss. Armando followed just steps behind and did the same. They were both greeting Catherine, when Victoria said, "Ya'll need to go turn on the TV in the den. You won't believe what happened last night."

"Why? What happened?" asked Armando.

"Just go turn it on. I'm sure they're still talking about it."

Armando did as he was told and walked into the den to turn on the television. Abbey looked puzzled at her mother and her friend. They could see the television through the pass through window. Sure enough, the morning news was still playing the same story she had seen earlier when Catherine had called to tell them what had occurred.

Abbey and Armando stood watching the news woman reporting the story about the murder at the gallery. They stood stunned. Abbey said to her mother, "Mama, that's awful! Poor Carlota. What's going to happen?"

Armando came back to the kitchen to pour himself and Abbey some coffee.

"Well, I'm sure the FBI is going to have to get involved. Now that there is stolen artwork, the risk of the sale of the painting to the black market, will surely require their two cents. For all I know, they might call my office and get me involved as well," said Armando.

He had barely finished his sentence when his cell phone went off. He excused himself and went into the next room to take the call.

"What about the girl that was murdered?"asked Abbey. "How does she fit into all this?"

"I was watching her last night," said Catherine with a displeased look on her face. "She was batting her eyes and flashing her big boobs at anyone that would look. Why I even saw her flirting with Mike Cunningham when he came in. Who knows how she got involved with whoever murdered her."

Victoria piped in, "Oh yes Catherine, you simply must call Mike and get the inside scoop. Why don't you have him come over and see what you can get out of him!"

"Oh it just so happens I'm one step ahead of you. He and I talked for a few minutes last night and we had made a date for later this evening before any of this ever happened. We decided to have one of our rendezvous because it's been a while for both of us, if you know what I mean? I intend to get a lot out of him all right."

"Oh, you are both impossible," said Abbey.

Armando came back to the kitchen and informed them that he had been called into the case.

"My buddy Rick Hatton from the FBI office just called and said we're on this case together. It seems they are going to be investigating along with the Carmel Police

Department. I'm, involved because they need a profiler on the case, so I'm headed downtown to the gallery now. They want us to get there before the body is removed so I have to go."

Armando leaned over and gave Abbey a quick kiss and said bye to the ladies. He winked at Abbey as he closed the door behind him.

"Have a seat for a minute, Abbey," said Catherine as she pulled out a chair from the kitchen table. Abbey poured coffee for all of them and took her seat next to Catherine, as they watched her mom start to peel peaches for her pie.

"Mama, are you stressed about something?" she asked as they watched Victoria go to town in the kitchen. "You always bake when you're stressed."

"Catherine, tell her about your visit to Madam Manon."

"Well Abbey, I told your Mama I went to visit Madam Manon a few days ago. When I was there, she told me that we were going to hear about a murder! And here it is! That woman knows what she's talking about."

Abbey sat back in her chair and looked at the both of them.

"I can't believe the two of you are still giving your money to that quack. This was just coincidence. You could have heard about a murder anywhere."

Victoria looked at her daughter and very convincingly said, "You can think what you want. But every time she's told us something was going to happen, it goes and happens Sugah'. You think what you want."

"Well ladies, I'm off to the office. We have a lot going on with all the buyers in town. Rite Monterey Realty is calling my name!"

Abbey stood and took her mug to the sink. She gave her Mama a kiss and waved at Catherine as she walked out the door to climb into her Mercedes and left. Victoria said to Catherine, "You just see what you can get out of Mike Cunningham tonight. I want to hear all he has to say tomorrow, and I want to hear all the dirty details too!" They both giggled like school girls.

18

It was close to noon when Armando and Rick arrived at the gallery. The traffic was now worse than ever. Camera crews were everywhere. The streets were crawling with people lining Ocean Avenue hoping for a peek, anything. The nosy shop owners were all outside. No one was in the stores. Everyone seemed to be on the sidewalk. Rumors were flying everywhere. Armando and Rick drove their SUV in to town through the back streets and double parked in front of the gallery behind one of the police cars.

Rick Hatton was the lead FBI investigator for the Monterey County office. He'd been with the service since graduating from college eight years ago. He had piercing blue eyes and was tall and strong looking. His blond hair cut military short. He had taken a liking to Armando during an investigation they had worked on together and they had become good friends. Even though the CIA didn't have an office in the area, they were allowed to use a small part of the Monterey FBI office as well as sharing all of the computer data equipment. Both departments cooperated with one another on many cases. This was a win-win for the taxpayers of the area.

Upon their arrival, they met Chief Cunningham. He gave them the basics of the crime scene and escorted them to the back room where Lindsay's body was still in place. The coroner was texting some information to his office and came up to greet them.

"Fellas, I'll be outside taking a smoke if you need me. We didn't want to move anything until you got here. I'm pretty much done with everything. We were just waiting on you. Let me know if I can answer any questions."

Rick and Armando put on some gloves and walked all the way into the room where Lindsay's body was.

"Wow!" said Armando. "I saw this chick here last night. I was here with Abbey and her mom. We went to get a bite to eat after we left around the corner, and I saw her flying in the door at the restaurant when we were leaving."

"Yeah? What do you remember?" asked Rick.

"Well, it's hard to forget the obvious," he said, pointing at her huge breasts. "But I was with Abbey, so I had to take peeks on the sly." They both smiled.

"No, what do you remember about her going to the restaurant?" asked Rick.

"Funny you should ask," said Armando. "I held the door open for her as she ran in and walked toward the bar. She was in quite a hurry. There was a guy sitting at the end of the bar she walked toward, but his back was to me. So I didn't get a good look at him. I remember getting a really weird feeling, but I brushed it off. I didn't have any reason to dwell on it, and I hadn't seen Abbey for a couple of weeks. I was more focused on getting her home. Let's just take a good look at her." Both men took pictures with their cell phones and looked closely at the room. They took pictures of the area around Lindsay, looking for any clues. She reeked of booze and cigarettes.

Armando got close to her face and asked Rick.

"What's that smell? Do you notice a smell other than booze?"

"No, not really. Just booze. What else do you smell? Can you pinpoint what it is?"

"It's a sweet smell. Faint, but definitely there. It's almost like almonds."

Rick bent over and sniffed. "Boy, she was pretty wasted. It's hard to smell anything other than the liquor."

Armando took out a pen light and pointed it inside her mouth. He didn't really know what he was looking for, but looked inside her mouth to see if there may have been something that could be causing that faint smell. But he didn't see anything.

"I'm going to take a look in the front at where the Picasso was. I'll meet you out there," said Rick.

Something was bothering Armando. He had that feeling he always got when his instincts were telling him to dig deeper at something. Those little hairs were standing up in the back of his neck that were always there when he didn't know yet what it was. But he knew he needed to pay closer attention. Some things made no sense. There were no puncture wounds on the body. There were no strangulation marks. The position of the body indicated that she may have been engaged in sex at the time she was murdered. All these things bothered him.

Armando went to the front to meet up with Rick. He had just finished looking at the notes the coroner's team had put together.

"Did you find anything interesting?" he asked Rick.

"No. Nothing that really jumps at me. I want to talk to the coroner outside, though. Are you about done in the back there?"

Armando shook his head yes and they both stepped out onto the street.

"So, any ideas what the cause of death is going to be?" asked Rick.

"Well, hard to tell right now. There don't seem to be any points of entry to the body, but I haven't looked at the body in totality. She could have a needle wound somewhere. Could be drugs, she seems to have had quite a bit to drink. Could be alcohol poisoning. I just don't know yet. It could be foul play, but until I know for sure, I hesitate to say. We'll get her to the morgue in Salinas and I'll open her up and do toxicology screen. A couple of the tests take a few days, but we'll have a better idea in a day or two. I'll give you guys a call as soon as I know."

Rick took one of his cards out and handed it to the coroner, thanking him for his time. They turned to Chief Cunningham and Armando asked:

"I'd like to take a crack at the owner of the Picasso if it's okay with you. Do you mind if we come along?"

"Not at all. In fact, if you fellows would like to take it from here, I'll just wait to get your reports. This is a bit out of my league. I'm sure you would agree. Just shoot me over some emails so I can keep up my paperwork. I'm afraid I'm going to have to be the bearer of bad news to Lindsay's mama. She went to Carmel High with one of my nephews so I've seen her around. She had a reputation you know. She was a real friendly girl, if you get my meaning. Here, I got the information about the Picasso's owner from the gallery owner before we took her home. She gave me this card. She's a real mess. Imagine coming in and finding not just having been robbed, but the body in her gallery too. She was a mess. I told her we'd talk with her in the morning. It's gonna take us a while to clean up around here. I don't want to disturb any evidence. I'll have another look around after they move the body. Let's talk later. Let me know what the owner has to say about his painting missing. His name is Colonel Ben Mackey. His address in Pebble Beach is there on the card. Good luck with the traffic going into Pebble. With the Concours going on, it's a real mess."

"Thanks chief," said Rick. "We'll be in touch."

The coroner was wheeling the gurney with Lindsay past them, and they stood and watched it go into van. Chief Cunningham went back inside, and Rick and Armando walked up the street toward their SUV.

"Where did you say you had dinner last night?" asked Rick.

"Actually, we're going to walk past it on the way to the car. But I don't think it's open this early in the day. I'm pretty sure they just do happy hour and dinner. We'll have to come back later. There, that's the place," said Armando as they walked past it from the opposite side of the street.

19

The traffic really was a mess. Armando and Rick decided to take the back entrance from Carmel Beach into Pebble Beach. It was a slow crawl, but eventually they reached their destination.

The houses on Palmero Way are some of the large original homes and big estates in Pebble Beach. Many of them were built by the fishermen who made their money when Monterey was big into sardines. The majority were Italian immigrants who worked hard and toiled while saving their money. They made wise investments in real estate all over the Peninsula. Now the homes have passed to the next generation, but many still have old money.

Colonel Mackey had inherited his home from his grandmother, who had married a wealthy doctor. He was third generation military man. His family also had old money.

Having served in Vietnam, he was a graduate of West Point. Now, he and his wife enjoyed retirement by playing golf and tennis. They were big in the arts community in Carmel.

The estate had to be reached by turning into an iron gate and following a long, winding driveway to the actual house. The rose gardens lining the drive were lovely. The estate was immaculately maintained. There were two gardeners pruning the trees as they drove in. The house was a light pink, two-story home with grand pillars on the front porch. There was an upstairs balcony above the front door from where you could see the entire garden.

As they drove up the circular driveway and pulled up in front of the house, an older gentleman came out to open the car door and greeted them.

"Good afternoon, gentlemen. Is the Colonel expecting you?" he said very politely.

Both Armando and Rick pulled out their identification badges and introduced themselves.

"It's possible Colonel Mackey is expecting us, but we don't have an actual appointment. Is he in?" asked Rick.

"Yes sir. He is in. If you will follow me, I will take you to him. Just wait in the foyer until I return."

The white-haired man left them just inside the front door. The home was obviously very opulent. A large round table sat in the middle of the foyer just inside the front door with a vase full of beautiful tall calla lilies.

There were twin half moon staircases that were placed on the left and right just beyond the point they were standing. They could see a grand piano near the window in the room to the right, and a comfortable sitting room to the left with a large fireplace. There were family photos on the bookshelves on either side of the fireplace. Both of them looked around and looked at one another. Rick said to Armando; "Sweet huh?"

Armando replied, "Yeah, must be nice."

A few minutes later, the old gentleman returned and asked that they follow him. As they walked behind the older gentleman, he took them passed the staircases, down a wide hallway lined with many paintings. He was obviously a collector of art, and had them displayed so they could be enjoyed. Many art collectors have their paintings behind locked doors and only showed them to special guests, and rarely at that. They reached a warming room with many windows and a breakfast table. The French doors leading to the back were opened. Outside on the patio sat a balding grey haired man and an older lady with short Lucile Ball red hair. They were wearing tennis clothes and drinking what looked like High Balls. It appeared as if they had just finished playing. The covered back patio was lined with flower boxes filled with colorful flowering bulbs. There was an impressive wide marble staircase that went down from the covered patio to a tennis court. Beyond that, you could see a gate that stood before a swimming pool. There were large shade trees on the back of the property.

"Gentlemen, I understand you are here from the FBI or something," said the Colonel as he dried the back of his neck with a towel. "I half expected you earlier than this. We obviously heard about the theft and murder at the gallery. Tragic situation. Very tragic."

Armando and Rick introduced themselves and showed them both their identification badges. The Colonel and his wife asked them to take a seat and offered them a drink, which they declined.

"This is a beautiful piece of property," said Armando. "It's so quiet. You must enjoy sitting out here hearing the birds sing."

Yes, we're really very fortunate. It's been in my family now for a couple of generations. The best part of it is that California passed a measure called Prop 13 in 1978 which has kept the property taxes at nearly nothing. It froze them at what they were at that time. If it wasn't for that, things would most certainly be different. But let's talk about why you are both here. I am aware that my Picasso has been stolen from Carlota's art gallery. But the most terrible thing is of course the murder of the young lady that works for Carlota."

Rick interrupted, "Well, we aren't one hundred percent sure there has actually been a murder yet. Although it looks like one. The coroner hasn't determined cause of death yet. We really can't discuss that part of the case you understand. We are here primarily to investigate the Picasso. Do you mind answering just a few questions?"

"No, of course not. Please, ask, ask."

Armando began the questioning. "Colonel, we couldn't help notice the paintings you have displayed in the hall as we were coming out here. Do you own many valuable paintings?"

"You might say that," said the Colonel. "My family and my wife Esther's family have been art collectors for several generations. We have inherited a few from both sides of the family. My grandparents both loved artwork. He was a surgeon in the Army before he went into private practice here on the Peninsula. He brought back that Picasso that was stolen, from an art dealer in Italy when he was in there after the war. Esther and I have added several pieces ourselves. We have used them as investments and plan on passing them on to our children and grandchildren when we are gone. The theft of this particular painting is quite disturbing. It's worth millions, you know. Even on the black market. I'm sure we have seen the last of it. Once these things are gone, they tend to stay gone. I'm sure we will work something out with Carlota about compensation, but the painting had great heart value to me. It was a wedding gift from my grandfather to us."

Armando then asked, "Why don't you have the rest of the art you have locked up? I mean, it's just out there for everyone to see? Doesn't that worry you?"

"My dear young man, art is supposed to bring joy to everyone. If it's locked up in a vault some place, how is anyone ever to enjoy it? Our collection includes a couple of Monets and Rembrandts as well as other valuable pieces. They hang on the walls all over our home. That particular painting has been on a wall in our bedroom since the night of our wedding. I'm sure you can understand our disappointment in losing such a large part of our life."

"Why would you lend such a precious item to someone? The risk is so great. Did it ever occur to you that something could happen to it?" asked Armando.

"As I just explained, art should be appreciated by everyone. Hording such pieces of work would be very selfish of us. Carlota is a reputable business woman. She has always run a very lovely gallery, and is always so very gracious to the members of the Art Association here in Carmel. Featuring the piece was very important to her during the Concours. We couldn't say no to her."

"Colonel," said Rick, "are you aware of anyone looking to steal artwork from collectors lately? Is this the kind of thing you would perhaps hear about in you circle or art friends and dealers?"

"Absolutely not. We haven't received any such warnings from anyone from any of the art groups we are involved in. We have many art collector friends and surely someone would have sent out an email or something warning the rest of us if this was the case. This has come as a complete shock to us. I mean, this is Carmel by the Sea and the Monterey Peninsula. Nothing like this ever happens here."

"One more question sir, ma'am, if you don't mind before we go. And I don't mean to ask with any disrespect, but do you have bills of sale for the paintings in your collection?" asked Armando.

"No offence taken," said the Colonel. "Of course we have papers for all of the works in our home. They are in the safety deposit box at our bank. Unless it's absolutely necessary, I'd like to wait until the Concours is done. I am getting crotchety in my old age and don't really like to drive around with as much traffic as we are having. Most of it should be gone by Monday. I can go to the bank at that time. Would that be all right with you?"

"Yes sir that would be fine," said Armando. "Here is one of each of our cards. Please call us if you have any concerns. If you send me an email or give me a call, one of us can come by and pick up the paperwork. It's just routine in our investigation you understand. Thank you both for your time. Good afternoon Colonel, Mrs. Mackey. We'll see ourselves out."

Armando and Rick shook hands with the couple and began their walk toward the front door. The gentleman, who had let them in, caught up with them just inside the French doors and followed them out, closing the door behind them.

"Nice pad," said Rick as they got in the SUV and drove off the property. What did you think?"

"Seems like a nice enough couple. Obviously very generous people. I really didn't get a bad vibe from either of them. I'd like to run them through the database back at the office when we get back. I'm sure they're clean, but just the same, I would feel better not leaving any stone unturned."

"Sounds good to me," said Rick. "Man, would you look at this traffic. Say, didn't you tell me Abbey's mom's boyfriend has a car showing on the 18th? Have you seen it yet?"

"No, I haven't. Seems like as good a time as any to drop by and take a look huh? Maybe some of this traffic will die down when it gets a little later. It'll help kill some time. How about I turn us in that direction? It's not far from here now."

"Let's do it!" said Rick with a big grin.

20

Armando turned in the direction of the Pebble Beach Lodge. When they got there, they asked to borrow one of the golf carts to drive out where the car was showing. It's amazing what people will let you get away with when you show them a CIA badge.

When they arrived, Paolo was just finishing a conversation with a couple who had a car showing near to his. They had been admitting the Bugatti, and asking him questions about her history. He excused himself when he saw Armando, and walked up to greet them. Armando introduced Rick to Paolo.

"Nice ride!" exclaimed Rick as he walked all the way around the car. The mechanic had taken the top down so people could look at the inside as well. He was always keeping watch and wiping off fingerprints and keeping her shiny.

"So Paolo, did you guys ever figure out the problem with the steering column?"

"No Armando, we have no idea how the inside wires could have gotten pinched. Perhaps in transit there could have been some movement, but it's highly unusual to have something like that happen. Even the steering wheel felt loose."

"Do you mind if I take a look at the column?" asked Armando.

"No, not at all. Please, sit inside. You too, Rick. Sit inside. I will take your picture, yes?"

Armando and Rick climbed into the front of the Bugatti and posed with big smiles. Afterwards, the two of them looked at the steering column for Paolo. They could see recent markings to the screws, as if someone had removed the screws to the steering wheel. The metal inside the groove that runs down the center of the screws appeared to have been recently disturbed. It was much shinier than the rest of the screws.

Armando asked Paolo, "Have you removed the steering wheel lately?"

"Why yes. My mechanic had to remove the steering wheel to find out why we weren't getting the correct movement. Why?"

"No reason," said Armando. "I can see the screws have been tampered with. I guess it's just my investigative mind. Is the steering working okay now?"

"Yes. It's working better now. Well, it's getting late. I have to meet Victoria back at the Lodge. I think we will be dining in tonight. We are both very tired from all of the activities from the week. Will you give me a ride back up?"

"Sure," said Rick as he got behind the wheel of the golf cart. Climb aboard. We'll drop you off. I have to have Armando take me to my car anyway. I left it parked at the Bureau office where he picked me up this morning. I think I'm going to call it a day."

The three of them waved at the mechanic and drove off.

Armando drove Rick back to the bureau office and went straight home. He was sitting at the kitchen table with the peach pie that Victoria had baked earlier that day when Abbey got home.

"That's not a good sign," she said to him. "Every time I get home and find you cleaning up a pie in your suit and tie, I know something is up. Can you talk about it?"

He shook his head no. "I'm trying to put some pieces together in my head and you know I can't resist one of your mom's pies. We've started the investigation on the death of that woman at the gallery. You know how I get when I'm in the zone. I'd rather not say anything until I have things tightened up. I have to go interview someone here in a bit. I don't think I'll be hungry for dinner, though. Do you mind if we just go to bed when I get back?"

"No, of course not. And I'm sure you won't be hungry after that!" she said as she pointed to the empty pie plate. "Will you be gone long?"

ARLENE GRACE

"No babe. I don't think so. I shouldn't be more than about an hour or so. Wait up, okay?"

Armando put the empty pie plate and took a drink of water from the sink. He turned and gave Abbey a kiss and a pinch in the tush as he winked and walked out the door.

He was headed downtown to interview the bartender at the restaurant they had been at the night before. The place was already crawling with folks getting dinner. The murder seemed to be the topic of discussion with everyone he could overhear talking. As he walked up to the bar, the bartender approached and said, "What'll you have?" He was a tall bald guy with piercings in his nose.

Armando pulled his badge out of his pocket and showed it to the bartender without trying to flash it too much as to not attract any attention to them.

"I'm Armando Shear. I'm an investigator with the CIA. I'm working with the police chief and the FBI on the investigation of the death that took place last night at the gallery around the corner. We know the woman that died was here last night with a man shortly before her death took place."

"Oh yeah, the chick with the rack. I couldn't help but notice her. Man, what a waste, huh? How was she killed?"

Armando looked at him as he put his badge in his pocket and took out a small notebook with a pen. "We aren't sure she was actually killed. The coroner hasn't released the cause of death yet. Can I ask you your name?"

"Sure, it's Dan, Dan Erickson." The bartender extended his hand to shake with Armando. "How can I help?"

"Well," said Armando, "you can start by telling me anything you can remember. Was she here with anyone?"

"Yeah, there was this guy who came in before her. I can't really remember how long before because I was pretty busy. There's a lot of people in town cause of the Concours and we were really jumping. When she got here, he started buying her drinks, one after another. I think they were drinking Scotch and soda to start, and then he asked for just the Scotch. He was getting her pretty wasted. I didn't think too much about it 'cause they looked like they were having a good time."

"Can you remember what he looked like?" he asked as he looked around the bar.

"Vaguely. I think he was wearing some kind of a dark jacket. I remember looking mostly at her whenever I could get a look at all. Like I said, I was pretty busy. He had dark hair and it was combed back. I think he might be somewhere in his forties. Hard to tell in here with the low light, too. I know he paid with cash when they left thought. He left a couple of hundreds on the bar and didn't even ask for his tab. It covered it and left me with a nice tip. I can't even tell you what time they left man, I was just really busy."

"Did you see him talking with anyone or did anyone else here talk with him?"

"No, I don't think so. He pretty much just kept to himself. He was looking at the TV screen at the news before she got here. After that, his face was buried in her neck the rest of the time. I didn't really get a great look at him. I'm sorry, man."

Armando asked if there were any cameras in the restaurant, and he said no. "There isn't ever much that goes on around here, you know?"

Armando gave him one of his cards and asked to be called if he remembered anything else. He thanked him for his time and walked out to his car. As he got in the car, he took out his phone and texted Rick to contact the newspaper and TV for any photos they may have taken of anyone who was at the gallery. Before he could get the car in gear, Rick texted him back.

"Already done, we'll have them in the morning."

Armando smiled and drove home. He knew Rick Hatton was on the ball. He was a good investigator.

21

It was about eleven-thirty that same evening when Carlota finally made an appearance downstairs. Gustavo was sitting on a recliner in the living room eating sardines when she walked in. She looked like a wreck. Her hair was all in shambles and she reeked of alcohol.

"What time is it?" She asked.

"It's about eleven-thirty," responded Gustavo. "I can't sleep. This has been an awful day. The news is crawling with all kinds of rumors about what happened. They say the coroner might call for an inquest to see what they can determine. He hasn't called it a murder yet. They haven't decided what she died from."

"Well," said Carlota, "murder or not, this isn't going to be good for business. I know I won't be able to go into that room again without picturing her laying there all dead. But murder or not, I don't know what I'm going to do about the Colonel's Picasso. How are we ever going to pay for that? I'm ruined as it is. "

"Well, the insurance should pay for that. Don't we have theft insurance?"

"Gustavo really, I haven't been able to pay the insurance for over a year thanks to you and your shit! We haven't had the money! Don't you understand? I haven't even paid the rent for months! I am ruined!"

"You don't have to speak to me that way. I didn't cause this by myself. I don't go out and have silk ladies' suits handmade in San Francisco. I don't go out and spend thousands of dollars on tacky jewelry and designer shoes for those size twelve boats of yours! Don't blame me entirely for everything. You have your vices, too!"

"You make me sick. You know I have to look presentable in our line of business. I don't see you in there every day trying to sell. You look like crap. I don't know how they let you into that classroom at the college dressed like a homeless person. You have no self pride. Let me know when the police chief calls. I'm going back to my room. I don't even want to look at you right now!"

"Well, at least you'll have the money from the Matisse."

He yelled back at her as she walked upstairs. But in the back of his mind, he was laughing. She was in for a rude awakening. In the morning, Gustavo left for Salinas. He went to several drug stores and a gas station to purchase Visa gift cards. He didn't want to take the chance of buying them in town in case there was anyone there who might recognize him and start to ask him questions about what had happened at the gallery. No one really knew him in Salinas. He also didn't want to buy just one. That might attract attention to him if he were to purchase cards for large denominations. He used some cash he'd stashed in his room from the sale of the last portrait he'd just finished. With all of the goings on, Carlota hadn't noticed that he had finished it, and hadn't asked him for the money he'd been paid for it. It was all he had, and he had budgeted what he needed for his escape. She made his blood boil. But he had to keep his cool especially now with all that had happened.

Gustavo had tried to call the number he'd been using to call Harry the Shark on. But it seemed to be out of order. He didn't really think he'd be able to contact him to ask him just what had really happened that evening with Lindsay. This was the kind of guy you asked to do a job, and after it was done; he didn't know you anymore. What had really happened to Lindsay, who knew? Although he felt like he was partially at fault, he knew he really wasn't to blame. He hadn't killed anyone. All he did was pay someone to steal a painting for him. That's all he could handle thinking about right now.

22

It was about nine-thirty in the morning when Captain Mike Cunningham began to back his vehicle down Catherine's steep driveway. She stood at the big picture window in front of her house waving at him. He could see her on the telephone, probably already calling her friend Victoria to brag about having ridden him all night like Yankee Doodle Dandy. He certainly hadn't minded. In fact, they had such a good time, they had made a date for the weekend to attend the Concours and get in some more riding lessons.

His cell phone rang, and he put the car in gear at the bottom of the driveway to take the call. It was Armando Shear.

"The coroner called to let us know the results of the autopsy. He couldn't find any puncture wounds on the body. Nothing that would indicate she had been injected with any drugs. There were no signs of strangulation, nor marks that would indicate that she'd been beaten up in any way. He did say though, that he had found a large amount of alcohol in her stomach, and something very strange. There were traces of Latex on her back teeth, like from a condom. He also found some small traces of a white powdery substance that wasn't yet dissolved. He sent them to an outside lab to see what it might be. His guess is that she had been engaging in oral sex, and may have ingested some kind of poison. He put a rush on that and the blood he sent them for analysis. There has to be something in her blood stream that wasn't in her stomach. My guess is that it's cyanide. He thinks it's possible too, but we won't know for sure until we get the toxicology report from the lab. I thought I smelled almonds on her breath when I looked at her at the gallery. My guess is that someone used her to get into the gallery after hours and poisoned her. If it is cyanide, she went quick and quiet. And if he put it on the condom, he is a real creep. Using her to steal the Picasso *and* get off.

"Interesting," said Captain Cunningham. "I guess we'll have to wait and see. I'm going to call the owner of the gallery and her brother in at about noon. Do you want to meet me there?"

"Sure. Rick and I will see you there by noon. I need to see about getting a guest list from her. Someone surely had to have taken some selfies or some other photos. I'm going to email you the pictures we were able to get from the photographer of The Herald Newspaper, and a small clip we got from the TV news. I'm hoping you can help identify some of the attendees, and maybe you can help in the interviewing. Someone had to have seen this guy that was with Lindsay at the bar after the party. I struck out with the bartender pretty much. He doesn't remember much more than Lindsay's boobs. He was too slammed and didn't really give this guy a second look. Do you know where there might be cameras posted on the street? Maybe a surveillance camera picked up something."

"No, Carmel doesn't have anything like that. Maybe some of the private homes, but not downtown. It's too Mayberry for any high-tech stuff. I'm on my way to the police department now. I'll take a look at your email and see what I can do. I'll bring you the names when I see you guys at the gallery. You can talk to the owner then.

"Perfect," said Armando. "See you there."

When Chief Cunningham arrived at his office, he went straight in. There were reporters in the lobby, and he didn't want to stop to speak to anyone. He told the officer at the desk that he didn't want to be disturbed. He first called the house and spoke to Gustavo, asking the two of them to meet him at the gallery at noon. Then, he opened his email to take a look at some of the pictures sent to him by Armando and Rick. They were hard to see, because there were a lot of people in attendance. Some of the faces in front of the pictures he recognized. The rest were really the backs of people. Others had flowers and things blocking their faces. He wrote down the names of the few he recognized or could identify, and put it in his pocket to give to them.

At noon, Chief Cunningham, Rick and Armando arrived promptly at the gallery. They were there before Carlota and Gustavo arrived but only by a few minutes. Chief Cunningham introduced them all to one another. Rick and Armando showed them their identification badges and asked if they would answer some questions.

Carlota answered the same questions for Rick and Armando that had pretty much been asked already by the police chief. She was still visibly shaken by the whole incident. Gustavo was nervous as well. His answers were followed by the nasty spit that flew from between his front teeth when he was nervous. Then, Armando produced some of the pictures they had from the night before. Chief Cunningham and Carlota were able to identify some of the guests, but not many. The pictures were too jumbled with the backs of heads and flower arrangements.

Chief Cunningham volunteered to go and question the guests he and Carlota identified. Armando asked for the information about the catering company. Carlota asked to go into the office to get the exact phone number to the owner. The place was still a mess as she walked into the back toward her office. She walked quickly past the room where Lindsay had been found dead. She didn't want to have to go in there, but knew it was inevitable. She would have to start to clean up as soon as the investigators left. She just couldn't leave the place in the condition it was in for very long.

When she entered her office, she walked toward her rolodex to find the card. Before leaving the room to give them the information, she quickly walked over to the basket of white tubes. She was almost afraid to find out that the Matisse was gone as well, but just had to know. She got the courage to go and shake some of them to see if they felt empty. The first few were, and panic started to crawl into her stomach again. But the fourth one she picked up felt like there was something inside, and rattled when she shook it up and down. Suddenly, she felt a flash of relief. She had at least been spared that problem.

Carlota handed Armando the card with the catering company information on it. He took out his notebook from his pocket and jotted down the name address and phone number.

Armando pulled a picture out of his jacket pocket and asked Carlota and Gustavo if they recognized the man in the photograph. It was a side view of a man holding a champagne flute up to his mouth. It was partially blocked by some other guest, but it was the only one Armando could find that showed someone fitting the description of the guy he saw sitting at the bar. Chief Cunningham didn't recognize him. Carlota said she had never seen him before. When Gustavo looked at it, he felt his hands shake. It looked like Harry. Thankfully, it wasn't a very clear picture. But he knew it was him.

"No, I don't recognize him. I've never seen him before," he told the inspectors. He wondered if he had sounded convincing enough. But he was still pretty shaken, and that helped make it more believable.

Chief Cunningham left to go talk to the locals he recognized in the pictures and some others he knew had been in attendance. Armando and Rick said their good-byes for now and left the gallery, advising Carlota and Gustavo not to open the place for business for a couple of days until things settled down a bit. They agreed.

Once they were left alone, Carlota and Gustavo went into the office. She went back to the tube that she had found to be the one holding the Matisse.

"Don't take it out of there," said Gustavo. "Let's just take a peek at it and make sure it's in there."

"Oh all right," said Carlotta." She pulled the top off barely exposing the canvas of the rolled-up painting inside.

"Thank God no one knew this was in here. I'd die if someone had taken this, too. Now let's get this place cleaned up. You go pick up the glasses and run the vacuum. I have to get the banking done so you can go to the bank. I'd better go through the telephone messages too. There must be a million of them. I have to start trying to contact someone to get rid of this painting. There are flowers in the room where Lindsay was. I don't want to go in there. Throw those out, too. I don't know what I'm going to say to the Colonel. But I'll worry about that later.

Go on now! Hurry up! Do as I told you!" She barked at Gustavo and sat at her desk.

Gustavo walked over to the room where Lindsay had been. Thankfully, he hadn't seen her in there. He didn't think he would have ever been able to walk in there again if he had. Carlota wasn't showing very much compassion for the dead girl. It was as if her death had become an inconvenience for her plans this week. Sure it was going to put a damper on some of the rest of the week's sales. But when was enough, enough? Gustavo felt terrible that Lindsay was dead. He still couldn't shake the feeling of guilt. But he knew he had to move forward with his plans for the future. Someone had lost their life. At least he had compassion in his heart. Now he worried that Harry would be identified and he himself would somehow be implicated. But for what? He didn't have the Picasso. And that's what it looked like. The theft of a famous painting. And he also knew that this wasn't Harry's first rodeo. Harry knew well what he did. And if he hadn't been caught up to now, the chances of his being caught in Carmel by the Sea were slim to none.

23

Armando and Rick couldn't catch a break. So far the only picture they had of the man who Armando considered could be the suspect was obstructed. It had been taken by one of the newspaper reporters. There were no cameras inside the gallery. The FBI lab couldn't identify any consistent nor significant fingerprints in the room Lindsay was killed. Carmel has no cameras on the street. It seemed they were striking out.

As they were leaving the gallery, Armando's phone rang. It was an agent at the office. He had emailed him a list that Armando had requested. They both walked to the SUV and climbed inside. Armando opened his laptop and checked his emails.

"What is it?" asked Rick.

"I asked one of the agent clerks to do some calling around to some of the hotels in the area. I asked him to get a list of the ones that had checkouts in the last couple of days. Particularly, the ones that had checkouts of single male guests. Most of them had been reporting mostly guests checking in. With the Concours and all the other events, most people were coming and not going. He found one not too far from here that had a man check out the day of the gallery event. It was a single guest who left late in the afternoon. Let's head over there."

"Geez Armando, that's why you get the big bucks. What hotel is it?"

"It's the Carmel Sunset Hotel. It's on Mission Street almost right behind the library. You drive. I'm going to call the catering owner and tell them we're going to drop by."

When they arrived at the hotel, they drove the SUV to the front and Rick gave the valet the keys but told him they wouldn't be long. He showed the young man his badge and followed Armando inside.

"We're looking for the manager on duty," said Armando to the older man behind the desk. There was a middle-aged woman nearby dressed in a dark navy blue suit. She overheard them talking to the elderly gentleman and stepped up to the counter.

"I'm the manager on duty. My name is Martha Wilson. How can I help you?"

They displayed their badges to the pair and Armando asked. "Did either of you take the call regarding the checkout of a single gentleman on Wednesday?"

"That would be me," said the older man. "I'm William Henry. I took the call. What's going on?" he asked.

"Mr. Henry, Ms. Wilson, we're trying to identify the man in this photograph. I know it's hard to see his face, but did either of you see him or someone that may have looked like the man in this picture? We think he may have been staying nearby."

Henry said, "I looked in the computer when I took the call. I didn't want to give out too much information because of privacy, you understand? I only told the man we had had only two checkouts in the last two days. One was a couple and the other was a single guy that checked out late on Wednesday."

Rick asked the man, "What can you tell us about him?"

"Well, not much. When he left, I was on the phone. He left his key on the desk with a twenty dollar tip. I didn't check him in. I really didn't get a good look at him."

"Can you tell us his name at least?" asked Armando.

"Let me see ... I'll look in the computer."

While Mr. Henry was checking, the manager, Ms. Wilson asked, "Can you tell me what this is about? Is this about the murder at the art gallery? We've never had any trouble here with any of our guests. I actually think I may have been the one to check him in. He came in late in the afternoon and the clerks were busy. I always chip in when I can to help them out. The picture looks familiar; it's hard to tell, though. It's only a side view of a man's face and it's taken from far away. The champagne glass in his mouth doesn't help either."

"Here it is," said Henry. "He checked in under the name Hap E. Gilmore. He was only here for three days."

"Actually," said Ms. Wilson, "he had reservations that he made online. I remember the credit card he gave me was a gift card. It had one thousand dollars on it. I ran it to make sure it was good, and it was. I figured he couldn't do too much more damage than that for three days, so I didn't ask him for more money. His stay was pre-paid when he made those reservations online, I think also with a gift card. The rest would have been covered by the one he gave me that day."

Mr. Henry was still looking in the computer and said, "He didn't have a car registered with the valet, either. He must have been hoofing it to wherever his car was parked. But there are plenty of parking lots around here."

Armando said to Ms. Wilson, "I'm afraid I'm going to need to take a look at that room. We need to see if we can loft some fingerprints."

"I'm sorry, but it has been cleaned. We do a very extensive cleaning to all of our rooms. The owners are physicians, and they have us clean first and then wipe everything down with Kavi Wipes, including the door knobs. They are real clean freaks. Those are surgical wipes and will kill anything! Besides, we already have a couple staying in there. They checked in late Wednesday night. I'm terribly sorry."

"I don't suppose you have any security cameras on the property, do you?" asked Rick.

"No, this is an older building. We've extensively remodeled the inside of the guest rooms, but the rest of the property is pretty much as it was built in the 1950s. Besides, the type of guests we have here are very exclusive. They command their privacy. Is there anything else?"

"Please take one of our cards. If anyone remembers anything else, just call either of us. Thanks for your time."

As Armando and Rick got into their vehicle, Armando told Rick that this had to be their suspect. It was obvious all he wanted was the painting. Lindsay's murder had to have just been a fluke. A sick fluke. He had to have been the one that poisoned Lindsay. She was his way into the gallery so he didn't have to worry about breaking in.

"Everything points to this guy. But he's pretty good at covering up his tracks. It's almost as if he doesn't exist. I mean, Hap E. Gilmore? At least he has a sense of humor. Let's get over to the catering office. I'll call in the name he used and have them run it. Let's see if we can pick up anything. But if he's paying in cash and using gift cards, we aren't going to get anything on him, I'm sure. This guy is a pro. He must have a buyer for that Picasso."

When Armando and Rick got to the catering office in Monterey, the owner had summoned the employees who worked at the gallery party. The bartender was a tall young man in his early twenties. There were two tray passers. One was a young, ordinary-looking woman, and the other was a young Asian man. They were all college students who worked part time while they were attending Monterey Peninsula College. They were led to a reception room where the owners usually met with clients to taste foods and cakes and make their reservations. They could tell these young kids were freaked out about the whole murder thing and at the thought of having been in the place where it happened. Armando and Rick asked them to try to identify the only photo they had. Both the men said no. But the young lady remembered seeing someone that she was pretty sure was the guy in the picture.

"He took champagne from my trays several times. I couldn't help look at him. He was very attractive. Almost pretty, for a man. He was wearing an Armani jacket and had a gold pinky ring. He kept looking at the girl with the boobs. I saw her talking with him a couple of times. I thought she might have known him or something. I didn't see him talking to anyone else."

"Did you get a good close look at him?" asked Rick.

"No, not really. I'm pretty shy and don't make eye contact with people. Especially good-looking men. But he looked too old for her, that's for sure. He was nice-looking, though. He looked like he had money. I watched him from around the room when I was passing the champagne."

"You mentioned he was wearing an Armani jacket. Are you sure it was designer?' asked Rick.

"Oh yeah, I'm studying fashion design. It was definitely Armani. He was dressed to impress."

"Get her name and her digits," Armando said to Rick. "I'm going to call the chief to see if he had any luck."

Armando thanked the owners and then walked outside to call the police chief. He told Armando that he had struck out with everyone he'd called on. No one remembers seeing the suspect. They only recalled visiting with the celebs at the party, or with friends. They all thought it was pretty tragic. Especially for Carlota.

At least now they had *one* person with information. One was better than none.

24

Armando and Rick went to the FBI office later that day. They had started putting up a war board together. Seeing all the information in front of him always helped Armando. Rick liked doing it the same way. That's the way he had been trained at the FBI. There was something about actually looking at all the facts and information right in front of you that helped in deciphering information. But in this case, nothing really seemed to fit. There was no connection to anything except to whoever killed Lindsay and the theft of the painting.

They knew by now that she had been the thief's ticket inside the gallery. Word was out throughout all the channels for the painting. More than likely, it would disappear. They both knew that whoever took the painting was going to sell it to a crooked art collector who would lock it up some place and no one would hear about it for years and years, if at all. The people who bought art in that manner had lots of cash and were very reclusive. They didn't care how or where the seller comes about obtaining a piece of art. All they care about is owning the piece of art.

"What do we really know about this Carlota Dominguez? Did you ask anyone to get information on her and her creepy little brother?" asked Armando.

Rick smiled at his friend and threw a file on the table in front of him.

"Here you are. Just ask and you shall receive," he said with a smirk on his face.

"I should have known," laughed Armando as he shook his head. "That's why you are the best," he said as he pointed at Rick.

"Oh, you say that to all the girls," laughed Rick. "No, seriously, I did some digging and had one of the guys check up on her the day we found out about all this."

Rick sat next to Armando and they began to look through the file at the same time.

"It looks like the little lady is in some serious debt. Her credit cards are all maxed out, and she recently closed her retirement account. The rent on the gallery hasn't been paid, either. It seems her brother had some gambling debts she paid off in Vegas. Some of the casinos have him banned from ever coming back. Their home is about to go into foreclosure. Looks like she had a lot riding on this gala event she just had. Do you think she could have set this whole thing up, with the Picasso?"

Armando scratched his head and said, "It doesn't add up. She didn't have an active insurance policy, so she owes money to the Colonel and his wife for the painting. If she had someone steal it, and then she tried to fence it, she'd lose the cash to them. And besides, she'd have to be a pretty convincing actress to fool me, too. I think this is just a tough luck thing with her. And her brother looks like he's too much of a wimp to steal anything. She's the brains of the operation, that's for sure. I think we can safely rule them out. Besides, she'd have to be an Oscar-winning actress to fool me. She was genuinely a hot mess that day at the gallery. He's just a creepy little guy with a big gambling problem."

Rick got up and started to write names on the board. He wrote the names of everyone they had spoken to or who was involved in the case. When he got to the Colonel's name, Armando sat back in his chair and asked Rick, "What about the Colonel? Do you think he could have paid someone to steal his own painting?"

"Why?" asked Rick with a puzzled look.

"Well, if they needed some money, this would have been a perfect opportunity to collect from the insurance policy. If they were to sell one of their paintings at auction, they may not get what they want for it. At least this way, they would collect the appraised value. I think we should keep him on the back burner and not rule him out just yet."

"Makes sense."

25

Carlota was on the phone in her office when Gustavo walked in. She had been on the phone making long-distance calls, trying to make contact with some of the people she knew from back home. She was hoping someone would give her the information she was looking for. They had been gone for a very long time. Most of the people they knew from their father's generation were gone or too old to remember them. She now had to deal with the family members and didn't know who to trust. Most of the children and grandchildren of the Nazi generation had become mainstream. They had left the crooked and illegal life style behind. But she was sure if she kept trying, *someone* would give her a lead. She sure didn't think it would be as difficult as it was proving to be.

"What are you doing?" asked her brother. "You look real tense."

"I'm trying to find someone to sell the painting to. All of dad's crook friends are dead. I guess the kids are like us. Just wanted to start fresh without any old ties to that kind of life. But there *has* to be someone. I know I'll find them. Where are the drug lords when you need them? Did you go to the bank yet? Do you have the deposit slip for me?" She barked at her brother with a scowled look.

"Here, I took the deposit to the bank just like you said. I went to the drive through so could avoid anyone asking me questions. As it is, the teller at the window went and told a couple of others tellers that I was there, and they came up to the window and were staring at me. I couldn't wait to get the hell out of there."

"Those nosy bitches! I have to stay here for a while longer. Go find something productive to do. I won't be home for a while. I guess we should open the gallery tomorrow. I just dread all of the nosy tourists that will probably come in just to see the 'place where the girl was murdered.' They won't buy anything; they'll just wander around and take pictures of the place for their Facebook pages. They are already taking their pictures in the front of the gallery."

"You shouldn't open until next week. Most of the people that are here for the Concours will be gone by then. Things will start to settle down after that."

"Maybe you're right," she said. "I won't open until Monday next week. Now, go home and leave me alone. I need to think and keep making more calls."

Gustavo glanced at the basket of white tubes next to Carlota's desk. He didn't want to bring up the painting. He was afraid it would occur to her to take it out for a look.

He decided to drive straight home and make his getaway arrangements. Now that he knew that she was looking to sell the painting in that much of a hurry, he really had very little time left.

Gustavo drove home and went straight up into his bedroom to use his computer. He knew he would have to go soon, but the timing had to be perfect. Just about everything had fallen into place. Lindsay's murder was the only think he hadn't bargained for.

After looking around the Internet for about an hour, he found a flight out of San Francisco airport, direct to Buenos Aires. He booked it using the Visa gift cards he had purchased in Salinas, so she wouldn't see anything if she got into his mail or if she looked at his bank statement. She was known to get into his private business all the time. She was nosy that way. He couldn't wait to make his move. Soon he'd be out from under her thumb, and away from all of her abuse ... *Soon*, he thought.

He sat for a little while longer and wrote another letter. He then drove to the Carmel Post Office and mailed it Express Mail.

He left there feeling nervous and excited at the same time. Gambling was second nature to him. But now he was gambling at something he wasn't sure would pay off.

26

Victoria and Paolo were meeting Catherine, Captain Cunningham, Armando, and Abbey for dinner. Tomorrow was the big day, the third Sunday in August. The day of the Concours de Elegance. They were meeting at a restaurant down the coast south of Carmel called Rocky Point. The restaurant sits along the coast on the rocks and has windows everywhere. The water is an azure blue, the likes of no other. The rocks along the coast are dark brown and jagged. They point outward from the water toward the sky, and host the splashing waves that constantly bathes them. Several times a year the whales migrate and can be seen as they swim north or south, depending on whether they are swimming south to give birth to their calves in the warm waters off of Mexico, or swimming north toward the feeding grounds off the coast of Alaska. The seagulls dot the sky, catching the last of the day's sun. The otters and sea lions bob gently in the water along the rugged coastline.

Victoria and Paolo pulled into the parking lot just before Armando and Abbey. When they entered the restaurant, they found Catherine and Mike were already seated at a table by the window. They had ordered two bottles of Napa Valley wine for everyone and had a head start.

As everyone took their seats, the waiter brought the menus and asked if anyone cared for something other than the wine. Catherine ordered some fresh calamari from Monterey Bay, and Victoria wanted to toast.

"Everyone get your glasses, I want to toast my darlin' Paolo. May he win Best of Show." They all clinked their glasses and began to comment on the beautiful day it had been, and how the weather was cooperating.

After they placed their diner orders, Catherine asked Armando how the investigation was going.

"Well, Catherine, you know I can't comment about that."

"You aren't any fun, either." Catherine said as she gave Mike a little pinch in the arm. "This one won't tell me anything. The only thing he'd tell me is that she was murdered all right. But that we can hear on the news. The coroner said she had ingested some kind of poison. But he wouldn't say what kind either. What's the big secret?" she asked.

Armando and the chief just shook their heads. Armando changed the subject and asked Paolo, "Have you ever seen a more beautiful sunset? Look at all of the colors."

In the middle of their meal, Paolo got a phone call. When he looked at the phone, he asked to excuse himself. He was gone for some time.

"Well, that's not like him," frowned Victoria. "He never takes phone calls when we are at supper. I hope everything is all right."

When Paolo returned to the table he asked to be excused for his temporary absence.

"I am sorry. I don't ever allow the phone to interfere with my personal life. But I recognized the number as one of my bank managers. It seems my son Roberto has gone on holiday and has been away from the bank for one week. He just told everyone he was going on a trip to Switzerland and no one has heard from him. I should probably get back home soon. I am very disappointed in him. I gave him a very important position and he has broken my trust. I called my other two sons and they haven't heard from him, either. Roberto is a good boy. But he likes to party, and he likes his women. He is not as responsible as the other two. I'm afraid I will need to go home after tomorrow, Bella. I should leave to go home with the car Monday morning."

"I'm so sorry Paolo. But I'm sure he's all right. You know how he likes to go on vacations with pretty girls." Victoria tried to console him.

"I'm afraid I gave him too much responsibility too soon. He just wasn't ready. It was my fault. He just wasn't ready for the responsibility. But let's not let this affect our evening. Tonight we celebrate. Tomorrow, we win!"

Paolo raised his glass for a toast, and they all continued to enjoy their dinner.

When Victoria and Paolo returned to the Lodge, she could tell he was still bothered by the phone call. She tried to take his mind off of it by luring him out onto the lovely terrace they had outside their suite. The evening was clear and the temperature was perfect. The light breeze was gently blowing through the pines, releasing their fragrant aroma.

In the distance, they could see the eighteenth fairway which now hosted the lovely automobiles that would receive their prizes in the morning, and beyond that, there were the tiny lights that twinkled from Point Lobos. The light of the full moon was reflecting on the ocean water. The soft sound of music was coming from the Lodge. It was light and romantic.

Victoria had gone in to change into a light pink satin teddy. Paolo loved lingerie. She stood by the wide brick railing and called out to him. When he stepped outside, he walked toward her.

"Come here, Sugah,'" she whispered softly to him. "I don't want you to worry about anything back home tonight. I'll fly home with you and I'm sure everything will work out just fine. He's just a young stud that still needs some tamin'. You just have to be patient."

Paolo picked Victoria up and gently put her on top of the brick railing. He took her face in his hands and kissed her gently.

"I don't know what I would do without you, Bella. You are what keeps me ... how you say ... grounded? I don't know what I would do without you right now. I know you are right, but a father who has also had to be a mother worries twice as much. Yes, please, come home with me. Besides, I don't want to be away from you anymore. We need to make plans to be together all the time very soon."

Victoria felt herself getting hot. He had a way of getting her motor running with very little effort. His Italian accent, the softness of his voice, the tenderness of his touch. It was any of the above, and it was all of the above. This was a man that women only dreamed of.

Paolo pulled her toward him and his excitement grew instantly. She began to unbutton his pants as he kissed her softly. It didn't take much effort to expose him, as he had become excited at her touch.

Paolo began to tenderly kiss Victoria on the side of her neck and slipped the thin straps of her teddy off of her shoulders, exposing her breasts. He kissed her shoulders and she crooned with excitement. Her head fell back and her hips slid forward. Paolo let his lips slide onto her breasts as he began to pinch and lightly tease them with his tongue. She began to feel hotter and stroked him faster.

"Oh Bella, I want you more every time we are together."

"Me too darlin', now stop torturing me and get in there!" she said, barely able to speak.

Victoria unsnapped the crotch of her teddy and Paolo was more than happy to accommodate her. He slid himself in and groaned with ecstasy. The brick railing had sat her up at just the right height. He was able to pull her toward him without any effort. Victoria wrapped her legs around Paolo as they began twerking in harmony. Her back arched further back and she put her arms around him, steadying him inside of her. Paolo was strong and resilient. He kept lingering without wanting it to end. Victoria loved that he was a slow and energetic lover. Most men his age were done in no time, leaving her without satisfaction. But he was her perfect match. They always finished simultaneously. It was as satisfying for each of them as they had ever experienced. And so they came, loud and explosive. They held each other in the moonlight until the moment passed, caressing and kissing one another tenderly, completely caught up in the moment. There were no worries now, just the thought of the Concours tomorrow and the excitement of the day that was to come.

27

Fog now covered the Monterey Peninsula, as is typical during the summer months. They say it's because the ocean water along the central coast is so cold that when the warm summer air hits it, it becomes a vapor that slowly creeps up from the bay. It creates a cool mist that slowly retreats back to the water usually by mid-day, leaving the sky open for beautiful, Mediterranean-like summer weather.

Armando had left the house around seven in the morning to take a run along the ocean at Carmel beach. Usually on Sundays, Abbey would come along, but this morning he decided to let her sleep in. She had a busy week at her real estate office and it had left her exhausted. Being the owner-broker placed a lot of demand on her time, and she had been putting in some very long days.

He had run the short block from their home Casa Brillantes which stood for Diamond House to run along the ocean on the packed white sand. It was an easy run. The sand made it a better run on than the concrete walkway along the ocean drive by the beach. Aside from a couple more runners, there was nothing else to distract him, and he needed some alone time to think about the case he was working on with Rick Hatton.

After much conversation with Mike, he still felt like facts about the case were leading them nowhere. There was very little evidence. The suspect was like a stealth airplane. No one really saw him, but everyone knew he had been there. Nothing really seemed to fit comfortably in his head. He still felt like something was missing and it was frustrating him.

The coroner was still going to hold his inquest, but it was really just a formality, mostly to appease the family of the victim. Really, they knew she'd been poisoned by ingesting cyanide while having oral sex with some sicko who had used her to get into the gallery. But something about the Dominguez pair was also bothering him. He just hadn't been able to put his finger on it. Nothing really seemed to incriminate either one of them. But usually his instincts were pretty dead on and he couldn't quite let it go just yet. He had told Rick that they were probably not involved, but something was still giving him that tingle he got on the back of his neck that was his gut signaling him to dig deeper. But into what? They knew about Carlota's financial situation. They knew there was a lot riding on the gallery event to get the siblings out of financial ruin. But there was still something he hadn't put his finger on. Something just wasn't right.

When he got back to his street, he finished by running all the way to the house. He found Abbey up in the kitchen making coffee.

"Hi sweetheart," she said with a sleepy smile. "You were up early this morning. Thanks for letting me sleep in."

Armando walked over to Abbey and gave her a big kiss. She pulled away. "You stink! Go take a shower."

"I will as soon as I have my coffee. I had a good run. The fog is out. It kept me cool. I needed some alone time to go over this murder case in my mind. Sometimes, it helps me to just be quiet and listen to the little voice inside my head."

Armando sat at the kitchen table and Abbey brought them both a cup of coffee. She took the seat across from his so she could look at him while they talked. She could tell something was really bothering him about this case. He was usually pretty good at pinpointing his suspects. But she could also see this time he was really struggling.

"So what did the little voice inside your head say?" she asked.

"It's pretty much telling me that there isn't much to go on. But I know there's something I'm missing about this whole thing. I suppose I just haven't found the missing link. I just have to be patient. In the end, I always figure things out. What time are we going to Pebble? Do you know what time your mom and Paolo are going to be there?"

"No, I'm not sure. I think Paolo has to be there early for the judging. They don't give out the awards until about noon. But the judges are out early. I'm not sure what time she'll be there. I'm sure she's going to take her time putting on her face today, though. There's going to be lots of people she knows there, and the photographers and all.

My guess is she'll probably get there around noon. I say we go take a shower and take it easy today. Maybe go back to bed for a while. We don't have to be there until early afternoon. Is around two all right with you?"

"Sounds good to me. Did you say something about going back to bed?" he said with a smile.

Abbey stood and started to run for the stairs.

"Last one there is a rotten egg!" she laughed. Armando stood and ran after her."

At the lodge, Paolo was stepping out of the bathroom in his robe with a towel just as there was a knock at the door. He had called for room service to bring juice, fruit, croissants, and coffee. He had timed his shower just perfectly to open the door. The waiter placed the cart in the living room by the dinette table. Paolo went into the room where Victoria was still asleep with a cup of coffee to wake her. They had both slept very soundly. Their lovemaking was always so relaxing. The patio door had remained opened through the night and had brought a nice cool breeze into the room.

"Good morning, Bella," he said as he sat on the side of the bed. He leaned over and give her a kiss. Victoria opened one eye and looked at him.

"What time is it? Is that coffee for me?"

"Yes Bella, the coffee is for you my darling. It 's about eight thirty. Come, put your robe on and have a little fruit with me in the other room. I'll need to leave here in a little while. I must be there when the judges come to see the other Victoria."

Victoria sat up and took a sip of the coffee.

"Mmmm, this really hits the spot. I think I may have had too much of my share of wine last night. I'm going to call the spa and see if they can give me a facial this mornin'. I don't want to scare anyone away."

Victoria put on her robe and took her cup into the other room. Paolo pulled out a chair for her at the table and she sat down. He put the fruit and the other items on the table for them.

"Oh Sugah', I don't think I'm going to be able to eat for a week. We ate so much last night. I may not fit in my dress."

Paolo laughed and put some fruit on their plates.

"Here, please eat some fruit. It's good for you. You need your strength. I need you at my side today. I don't know any of these people. Besides, you must be at your best for all of the pictures that will be taken of the most beautiful woman at the Concours."

"Oh Paolo, you know just what to say to a girl to make her blush."

"I'm going to be leaving in about half an hour. I want to be there for the judging. I'll just stay and visit with some of the other car owners. I'm sure they will all be there today. I haven't had a chance to really walk around and look at the other cars. Do you think you'll be out there by noon? I have a picnic planned for us. The lodge is going to bring our basket out at that time."

"Oh Paolo, you are so wonderful. Of course I'll see you there at noon. Now let me go take my bubble bath. You be sure and put on the tie I got you that matches my dress. We want to look our best!"

Paolo walked out of the lodge after they finished their breakfast and he got dressed. Along the walkway, there were golf carts lined up for the convenience of the car owners who were guests there. They were ready to drive them out to their vehicles.

Although it was a long walk, Paolo decided he would walk instead. He looked very dapper in his white suit and powder blue shirt. He also wore the silk blue and light pink tie Victoria had given him as a gift to bring him good luck today. It matched the summer dress she was going to wear. It made him look very European.

He was still troubled by the phone call about Roberto, but he didn't want to ruin the day for Victoria and all of their friends. As soon as he got out to the car, he would call from his cell phone and make arrangements to have the car picked up immediately following the day's events and taken to the airport. He would fly home with it the next day instead of taking a separate plane. He had such mixed feelings about today, but decided he was going to enjoy such a spectacular event. He would worry about Roberto tomorrow.

28

$\mathcal{I}$t was close to eleven when Gustavo got up to go downstairs. He made coffee and went outside to get the newspaper. He was reading at the kitchen table when he heard Carlota stumbling down the stairs.

"Did you make any coffee? I need some coffee. I slept too hard."

"You shouldn't take so many of those pills, as much as you drink."

Carlota walked over to the coffee pot and poured herself a cup. She took a seat at the kitchen table next to her brother and took a sip.

"This tastes bitter. Do you think it tastes bitter?" She walked over to the cabinet and pulled out a bottle. She poured liquor into the coffee cup and took another taste.

"There, that's better. You want me to sweeten up your cup?" she asked. She looked like hell. Hung over from the night before, she was getting an early start on her drinking today.

"Well, I think I have a lead. I got hold of Ursula Shultz. Do you remember father's friend Karl Shultz? Well, this is his daughter-in-law. She gave me a name of someone in New York that is an art dealer that buys art like on the side. She said he might be interested in the painting, or might know someone that could help us. I left a message on the man's phone last night. I had to be very careful with what I said, you know? I'm waiting for a call back. I hope it will be today. I think I will just stay around the house today. Rest is what I need today. You should find something productive to do. When was the last time you cleaned up the garden? The front of the house looks like shit."

Gustavo's blood began to boil. He looked at his sister across the table and pictured himself grabbing her by the neck and squeezing the life out of her. But that would be too quick. He wanted her to die a rotten death.

He put the newspaper under his arm and went up to his room to finish reading it. Not long after that, he heard her stumble up the stairs again and slam the door to her bedroom. He decided just to take a drive down to the Monterey Wharf to get some fresh air. He needed to get out of the house and away from her. Sitting on a bench by the walking trail was always a good distraction on a Sunday. There are always lots of interesting people walking by or riding their bikes. In any case, anywhere was better than being in that house with her. There was nothing else he could do now but wait until his upcoming trip.

At noon, Victoria arrived by golf cart to the eighteenth fairway at the Pebble Beach Golf Course. She made a grand entrance in her lovely pastel flowered dress and big floppy hat. Everyone who had already arrived was dressed like they were going to an afternoon tea party. It was the event of the season. Champagne was everywhere and everyone was anticipating the judges' awards.

Most of the ladies wore big sun hats and pretty dresses. The gentlemen were dressed handsomely in sport coats or jackets. Everyone was enjoying the beautiful day. The weather couldn't have been more delightful. The view of Carmel beach was spectacular.

Catherine and Mike had already arrived and were standing next to the car, talking to Paolo. The Bugatti was surrounded by astonished car buffs who had never seen anything like her.

"Catherine, let's get inside and have our picture taken. Come on Sugah' get in with me. Paolo, darlin', please take our picture."

Catherine grabbed a couple of champagne flutes from a passing waiter and the two ladies climbed in. They stood clinking glasses as their pictures were taken. Then, Victoria spotted the judges headed their way.

"Paolo, look there! The chairman and the judges are comin'. They're headed our way!" she said, squirming with excitement.

A heavy-set man in a straw hat and three others walked up to the car and asked; "Who is the owner of this great beauty?"

"That would be me, sir. I am Paolo Marcello, the owner."

"Well sir," said the gentleman, "it is with great pleasure that we present you with the award for Best in Show for this year's Concours de Elegance."

The man shook hands with Paolo. Everyone in the area applauded. Catherine and Victoria climbed out of the car and went over to give Paolo a hug and to congratulate them. Victoria was screeching with delight.

One of the men put a huge ribbon on the windshield of the car and another handed Paolo a beautiful trophy. The judges had their pictures taken with Paolo and the car. They thanked him for bringing the Bugatti all the way there and extended him an invitation for the following year. More people came toward them to take pictures of the car and to congratulate him. They were all full of questions about the history of the car and its origin. Before they knew it, an hour had passed and their picnic lunch had arrived.

Paolo and Victoria, along with Catherine and Mike, were sitting on the lawn near the car when Abbey and Armando arrived. They saw the ribbon on the windshield and walked over to congratulate Paolo. Victoria asked them to have a seat on the blanket beside them and she poured them each a glass of champagne for a toast.

"You see? I told you she'd win. She's named after me. She had to win! Why it's the most beautiful car here. Let's toast to next year. You have to come again next year again, Paolo. Wasn't this fun?" They all raised their glasses and toasted Paolo.

"What car are you going to bring next year, Paolo?" asked Catherine. "Do you have one named after me?"

They all laughed.

By about five in the afternoon, the crowds had begun to thin. Victoria and Paolo decided to call it a day.

When everyone had gone from the fairway, Paolo and Victoria decided to return to the Lodge and have dinner in. The sun and all of the excitement had tired them out. When they arrived at their suite, they found the room filled with fruit baskets, wine baskets and beautiful flower arrangements congratulating Paolo for his trophy win. They decided to strip down and sit in the hot tub out in the patio and unwind. The water was steaming hot, and felt great to both of them. It was nice to finally relax after such a long and exciting day.

"Bella, I have made arrangements to have the car taken back to the airport tonight. I am trying to get clearance for the plane so we can leave tomorrow afternoon. If you are coming with me, you must go home in the morning and pack."

"Of course, Sugah'. I'll go home first thing tomorrow and throw a few things together for the trip. I need to do some shopping anyway, so I promise not to overload the plane with all of my usual suitcases."

Victoria could tell he was still troubled. She didn't know if she should bring Roberto up or not. She decided to let sleeping dogs lie. Instead, she continued to bring up the events of the day to distract him and keep him happy. They sat out under the stars for hours before retiring to bed. Tomorrow was going to be a busy day.

29

Carlota woke up with a slight pain in her chest and a headache that wouldn't quit. She tried turning her pillow over. Then she tried tossing and turning, but nothing seemed to help. It was too early in the morning and she didn't want to get up. She dismissed the chest pain to the tremendous amount of stress she was in and decided to get up and look for some aspirin or acetaminophen.

When she threw her blankets off, she stood up and made her way to the stairs. She had to hold on to the hand rail and steady herself with the wall to get to the bottom.

As she got to the kitchen, she noticed there was no coffee made. She knew Gustavo was still in his room asleep.

That lazy good for nothing jerk. What a life! Sleeping and gallivanting with no responsibility, she said under her breath.

She began to look through the drawers for something to take for the headache. There was hardly anything there. She could only find a bottle of ibuprofen with one pill inside and an almost empty bottle of the Xanax that she had been ingesting like candy for the past two or three months.

That will have to do, she thought as she twisted the cap off and poured the last two pills into her hand.

She walked over to the sink and poured herself a glass of water, then noticed the dishes that had been left for what seemed like a week. This made her furious, but she was feeling too crappy to walk back upstairs to wake Gustavo and give him a good screaming to right now. She just wanted to make some coffee and see if it helped her feel any better.

After turning on the coffee maker, she sat at the kitchen table to wait for the coffee to brew. It was the first time she'd had in the last week to soberly and quietly think about everything that had transpired.

She decided to send Lindsay's last check to her mother with a card. It was the least she could do. And she was also anxious to hear back from the man she left a message for regarding the painting.

When the coffee was ready, she poured herself a cup and sat back down at the table. The chest pain was subsiding, but the headache was killing her. She put the cup up to her mouth but stopped to take a deep breath, and enjoy the aroma before she took her first sip. It smelled unusually good to her. Probably because she had been going a hundred miles an hour for the last few days and hadn't even had the time to devote to enjoy a simple cup of coffee. It dawned on her that she couldn't remember the last time she ate anything, either. She'd had a few bites from the food she served at the gallery, but even that she had scarfed down in a hurry.

She stood and opened up the fridge. There was a half used loaf of bread, three eggs, some chocolate syrup and butter. Nothing she could eat without effort. Gustavo usually ate on the run, ordered pizza, or ate sardines. She could never figure out what this love for sardines was all about. She remembered her father eating them out of the can when they were young, and supposed he had probably developed a taste for them then.

After a second cup of coffee, she decided to go upstairs and get dressed. She was afraid she would miss the call from the art dealer since she'd used the gallery's phone to call him. She didn't want to use her cell as to avoid any suspicion. Out-of-state calls were common at the gallery from art brokers and buyers.

Once back in her room, she picked out a suit to put on and she got in the shower. It seemed that the headache was better with the hot water pouring on her head. But soon, the hot water ran out and she had no choice but to step out dry off and finish dressing. Not much makeup, and not much to do with her hair which she always wrapped up in a bun, she was ready in no time.

She decided she didn't want to deal with Gustavo this morning. She was still disgusted about the dishes in the sink. She just got in her car and drove down Ocean Avenue and found a parking place near the front door of the gallery. Most of the traffic from the Concours was gone or going. Few people were out on the street at eight thirty in the morning. Most of the shops didn't open until nine-ish or ten-ish.

As she walked to the front door, she heard a car slow down behind her.

"Hey Carlota, you're out early this morning," said Captain Mike Cunningham. "You mind if I come in with you for a few minutes?"

"If you must," she responded, and walked in leaving the door open for him.

When he stepped inside, she was walking around turning on the lights.

"You planning on opening for business today?"

"I haven't decided yet. I'm not feeling very well, but I have some things I have to take care of. So here I am."

"Why don't we go into your office for a few minutes? I really didn't get to talk much with you the day ... well, you know ... that day."

Carlota turned and walked in the direction of the office. She opened it and turned on the light, taking a seat at her desk. Captain Cunningham followed and sat on a chair beside her.

"First of all, you have to know how sorry I am this happened to you and your brother. Especially on such a busy week for you. But I need to ask you some questions that I don't want you to get offended by. You know it's my job. The City of Carmel pays me to keep everyone safe, and I feel this puts a black mark on my record. So I have to exhaust every effort to find out what happened to Lindsay, and make sure you are safe here in your business as well. For all we know, this is something that may repeat itself. We have a lot of art galleries here in town, and if we have an art thief, the sooner I get my hands on him, the safer everyone is."

Carlota sat looking at Captain Cunningham and her eyes widened.

"I never thought about that! I guess you could be right.

This could be a predator stalking art galleries. Oh dear! It never occurred to me that way!"

"Now Carlota, you and I have known each other many years. Now, I've had to do some digging around and so has the FBI and that CIA fellow. We know you've been having some financial difficulties lately."

"You don't think I had anything to do with the theft of the painting, do you? And I certainly had nothing to do with the murder!"

Carlota began to turn red. She could feel her pulse in her temples. Her breathing became labored. The thought of anyone finding out she was broke was devastating to her.

"Now calm down, I'm not accusing you of anything, but I have to ask the questions, and I have to have answers for when I write my report. If I don't, I'm not doing my job. Have you had some money problems lately?"

Carlota was so embarrassed she wanted to die. She knew she had to answer his questions, but didn't want to.

"Yes, it's true. I'm pretty much broke. Gustavo has always had a bad gambling problem, so I forbade him to go to Las Vegas any more. Well, little did I know, he started to gamble online. Poker; he loves poker. Well, he maxed out our credit cards, he cleaned out our savings. I haven't even been able to pay rent for months, and we're about to lose our house. I was really counting on this week to help with the cash flow. And now *this* had to happen! If I had wanted to kill anybody, it would have been him! Do you know how screwed I am? I didn't have the money to pay our insurance here at the gallery. I'm going to have to pay the Colonel for that Picasso! I don't know what to do!"

Carlota began to sob. Captain Cunningham decided he was going to stop with the questioning and just leave. He'd gotten the answers he needed. She'd been painfully honest with him and he told her he would keep her confidence and not discuss her private situation with anyone in town.

Carlota thanked him and walked him to the door. She locked it behind him. Now, she had to worry about a serial thief and killer possibly being in town.

In the background, she heard the phone ringing in her office. She ran toward the back hoping to catch it before whoever was calling hung up.

"Hello, this is Carlota Dominguez. Who is this?"

"Miss Dominguez, you left a message on my phone yesterday about a painting. You should be careful who you leave messages like that for, you know?"

The voice was that of a man with an accent. It was deep and raspy.

"So, you got a painting you want to sell? Matisse, huh? Where'd you get this painting?"

"I bought it from a dealer in Italy. I bought it as an investment and I need the money. Will you take a look at it? Do you think you might have a buyer for it?"

"Well you know ... I won't be sure until I see it in person. I'm in Chicago on business right now. I'm from New York. I can run it by some of my people. Do you have a picture?"

Carlota thought for a minute, and remembered she still had the original email that was sent to her with the picture of the painting.

"Yes, I can send you an email with the picture. Can you give me an email address?"

"I'll take a look and see what I can do. If I gotta fly to Cali, I'd rather do it from here. I'm halfway there. Let me take a look at it and I'll call you later this afternoon. Are you going to be there?"

"Yes, yes. I'll be here. I have some business to take care of. What time will you call?" she asked nervously.

"Give me a break. I told you, I gotta take a look at it first and make some calls, but I'll call you later."

Carlota hung up and opened her computer to look for the email. She realized that it hadn't been very smart of her to keep the communication. But she was glad she hadn't deleted it. But she made a mental note to put in the trash bin after this whole thing was over. She didn't want anyone finding it and implicating her in any way. She was in enough hot water as it was.

30

Victoria and Paolo had finished packing their things by noon. He went to the lobby to take care of the bill and she waited for the bell boy to come take the suitcases and put them in the trunk of her BMW.

She slid in the driver's seat and he walked out to meet her. As they were driving out of Pebble Beach toward her Carmel home, Paolo was taking a last look around.

"This is really a beautiful place, Bella. No wonder you don't want to move away permanently."

"Well Sugah', we can always live half the year here, and half in Milan. That's a beautiful place, too."

In no time, they were pulling into her driveway. Paolo opened the trunk and put his suitcases in the garage, then he took Victoria's into her bedroom.

No one was home. Armando and Abbey were at work. That gave them privacy and time for Paolo to complete making the arrangements for them all to fly out. He had to wait for clearance from Monterey Airport. They had a large number of private planes leaving, and he hadn't scheduled a flight plan with them. He'd originally planned on sending the car home Tuesday, and hadn't been in any hurry to leave himself. The day after the Concours was always a busy day at the small airport. They had to give flight clearance to the private jets in between the regular commercial airline traffic.

Victoria was in her room, thrashing through her walk-in closet, throwing things on the bed. Paolo stood at the doorway, shook his head and decided he didn't want to be any part of that mess. So he went into the den to watch TV until they got word.

His cell phone rang, and it was the master at the airport wanting to confirm a nine o'clock take-off time. Paolo told him they would make that time work. He then called the mechanic and asked that he be at the airport to meet the car and make sure it was secure for the trip. He told him that they were all leaving for Italy at the same time.

Paolo walked into Victoria's room to tell her the news about the departure time.

"Sugah'," said Victoria, "Do you think we'll have time to meet Abbey for a late lunch? I just called her from my room and told her I thought we'd be leavin' tonight. She has a function to go to after work and won't be home until late. I'm afraid we'll miss her and I really want to see her before we go."

"Of course, Bella. You can finish packing later. We don't have to be at the airport until seven-thirty this evening."

"Thank you darlin'. I'll call her and tell her we'll meet her at the wharf. Her choice on the restaurant and ask her what time she can get away. It's getting' late already, so we should go now if she can get away."

"Sure my Darling. Whatever you say. I'd love to go to the Monterey wharf before we go anyway. I haven't been able to spend any time down there on this visit. We've been so busy with all of the activities in Carmel. Call her and tell her we're on our way."

Victoria pranced back into her room to get a hat and to call Abbey. They left to meet her in thirty minutes. Victoria wanted to kiss her baby girl before she left town.

Captain Cunningham called Armando and Rick after he returned to the police station. He called to fill them in on his conversation with Carlota and to let them know he was going to write his report, updating the file on the case. The coroner had already had his TV press conference that morning declaring Lindsay's death a murder, so he felt he needed to comply with his paperwork. He also discussed the possibility of the murderer still being in town.

Armando and Rick didn't think that was the case, but left him to his own investigation. It was his town and his prerogative, if he really wanted to continue to be cautious.

After all, there is always the possibility of there being a copy cat thief, hopefully not another murder. Armando and Rick were at a dead end. Not being able to get much of an identification on the suspect, all they could do now is hope someone else from the public would come through with new information. They would have to let this case steep for a while. Things sometimes just take time. And time they had plenty of.

The Colonel had dropped off the receipt of purchase he had in his vault, from when the Picasso was given to them as a gift. He'd been there first thing in the morning as he said he would be. Now it was just a formality authenticating the paperwork. But it seemed to be in order. It was chill time. Nothing more they could do right now but wait. Armando knew things would unravel soon. He just felt it.

31

Carlota had been trying to keep busy in her gallery. She'd decided to leave the doors closed. There was a lot of packing up of paintings and sculptures for shipment that had been purchased at the gallery the night of the big event. In the process, she had decided to re-arrange some of the other items that were left, to give the gallery a new feel for when she reopened.

Usually, she would have Lindsay or Gustavo help. But she didn't want to be around Gustavo right now. She was waiting for that call, and didn't want him there.

Carlota was in her office sending emails to some of the artists who usually placed their work in her salons for sale on consignment. She let them know that she plenty of space for display, since her show had pretty much been a sellout. She needed new art to fill the walls and the rooms that would be empty once she finished packing everything that had sold.

She sat at her desk to call FedEx and make arrangements for a large pick up in the morning. She wanted them to come after all of the pieces she was mailing to their new owners. Then, the phone rang. It was the art dealer from Chicago.

"So, hey Carlota," said the raspy voice on the other end of the line. "I made a few calls about the painting, and, yeah, I might have a couple of possibilities. I wanna come out and take a look at it in person and talk price witcha. So I can take the red eye outta here tonight and get into San Jose Airport in the morning. I guess it's what, about an hour to your place from there?"

Carlota's hands began to shake. She felt sweaty and her heart was beating against her chest.

"Yes, well, maybe an hour and a half. It's not too bad. Oh, I really appreciate this. I promise you won't be disappointed. What time should I expect you?"

"Well, I'll get in some time around eight. I'll rent a car and get something to eat. I think between eleven and twelve. How's that sound?"

"Wonderful!" she said with a bit too much excitement in her voice.

"I'll see you then."

Carlota hung up the phone. Her hands were shaking and she was nervous and relieved at the same time. The sooner she got rid of the painting, the sooner she could try to get some of the debt paid off and get back on track.

Her nerves were starting to get to her again, so she pulled open the right side desk drawer, and pulled out a bottle of whiskey she kept in there. Then she dug in her purse for her pill bottle. She emptied two Xanax onto her hand, and swigged them back. She needed to keep herself calm so she could finish everything she needed to get done before tomorrow.

She made arrangement with FedEx to be there at nine in the morning so all the stuff would be gone by the time he arrived. She wanted her time with him to be without any disturbance. Complete privacy was of upmost importance.

Carlota worked feverishly throughout the day packing and addressing everything in the gallery, stopping only occasionally to down more whiskey and some of the left-over hors d'oeurves that had remained in the fridge from the event. In between, she took more Xanax. She needed to steady her nerves. She would shake from lack of alcohol, so she would take the pills to counteract the ups and downs of drinking. She wasn't really keeping track of the amount of pills she had been taking. She'd been too focused on what she was doing to bother.

By ten o'clock, she had finished with everything, including answering emails in between packing, and returning some calls from some of the buyers who had left her messages expressing concern, for what had occurred in the gallery. She was exhausted so she decided to call it a day.

On her way home, she stopped by the liquor store and purchased a case of vodka and a case of whiskey. Some she would leave in her car to take back in the morning to the gallery. The rest she would take into the house.

When she arrived home, she opened her trunk and took out one bottle of whiskey and vodka each to take inside. She found Gustavo in his art studio with the TV on.

"What have you been doing with yourself today? Nothing, I suppose?"

Gustavo looked at his sister, standing at the doorway with the two booze bottles in her hands. He was nervous.

Tomorrow was his big travel day, and he didn't want to say or do anything that would tip her off to any of his plans.

"I got a call from some people down the coast to do a portrait," he said.

He was lying. There had been no such call. He just wanted to justify some of his time and get her off his back.

"They are coming tomorrow to see the painting. I have a man coming from Chicago to see it in the morning."

Gustavo felt his face flush.

"Tomorrow, that's good. Tomorrow is good."

Carlota turned and walked up the stairs to her room. He heard the door close and the lock turn.

Just in the nick of time, he thought. *I'm leaving just in the nick of time. A day later and I would be screwed!*

Gustavo went upstairs. He waited until he could hear the usual snoring sounds coming from her room. He sat in front of the TV, watching the evening news and waited.

He knew she would be in there boozing it up and popping pills to go to sleep. He had to be very quiet now.

After about an hour, Gustavo heard the ever familiar sound of her throat-gurgling snoring. He turned the TV down a bit, and went into his closet. He took out the small soft-sided suitcase that had been buried in the back of his closet, and the white tube he'd stashed with the Matisse inside since Harry dropped it off in the mailbox.

There was only so much room in the carry on, so he had to be smart. He first placed the tube inside, on the bottom. He took out some underwear and a couple of pants. Then he picked out a couple of cotton shirts to take. He planned on getting all new things once he sold the painting in Argentina. New things for a new beginning. That's the way he was going to roll. He knew he'd have plenty of money to live on for a lifetime, as long as he didn't gamble it away. But he'd promised himself he was finished with that.

Gustavo took out his best suit and put it in the front of his closet, where he could get to it in the morning. This was an important trip to him, and he wanted to look his best. Then, he went to his computer and printed his boarding pass. He put that inside of his suitcase as well.

Now, he was going to try to get some sleep. He was equally nervous and excited at the same time. He laid there thinking about all the final details that had to be done before he left. Making a mental note of everything, he finally slipped into sleep.

32

Gustavo was awakened by the sound of the garage door. His room sat directly over the garage and the door always made a loud bang when it closed.

Carlota had left. He looked at the clock and discovered it was almost nine. He jumped out of bed and stood there, not knowing what to do first. He tried to calm himself.

First, he went downstairs to see if she was really gone, or if he had dreamt it. Looking in the garage, he was relieved to know she had indeed, actually left.

Pouring himself a cup of coffee, he took it upstairs and took his time taking a shower. He shaved as closely as he could. It was going to be a long trip and he wanted to look good when he got there.

When he went to get dressed, he went to look for a pair of socks and realized he had forgotten to pack some.

So he dug around until he could find a few pairs that didn't have holes and slipped them into the front zipper compartment of the suitcase.

Before he put on his suit, he had decided one of the things he wanted to do, was erase his search history from his computer, just in case Carlota decided to go snooping around his stuff when she got home. He knew she would flip out when she realized he wasn't coming back, and would go searching for clues as to where he might have gone.

After thinking about it, he decided he would just take the laptop with him. He had just enough room in the bag to stick it in on the side. It was small, and didn't take up that much room.

Taking one last look at himself in the mirror, he took one last looked around his room, the room he had felt imprisoned in for the last fifteen years. He was so glad to be leaving. He had no regrets.

Once he reached the kitchen downstairs, he went into his art studio to retrieve some of his favorite brushes to take with him. He had a sentimental attachment to a few. Many artists are soft that way. He had also decided to leave Carlota a note telling her he would never be back. What better way than to put it on canvas.

Gustavo placed a large canvas on his easel, and squeezed out some black paint onto his pallet. He had planned what he was going to say, and began to paint his message while laughing out loud. He was getting great pleasure writing his last message to his sister.

When he got in his car, he drove downtown and used an ATM machine to withdraw the rest of the money he had in his checking account. He also had with him some of the leftover money from the last portrait he had done and had managed to hide from Carlota. That would have to help get him through customs and get him by until he could sell the painting. He knew he was going to need a couple of Ben Franklins to bribe the customs officers with so they wouldn't ask too many questions when they saw the painting in the tube. That usually worked fine in Argentina. Most of them were on the take. He didn't anticipate any problems.

Once he was done, he got on Highway One and headed for San Francisco to board his plane. He had plenty of time and wasn't in any hurry. What's done is done. His chest felt lighter. He felt like he was able to breathe in a way he hadn't been able to breathe for years. No more pressure from Carlota. No more abuse or belittling. He was free. He just hoped everything else he had planned would go his way. But he was confident.

Once he parked at the airport, he threw his keys inside the car. After all, he wouldn't need it any more. Then he went inside to check in to wait for takeoff.

33

Carlota arrived at the gallery just in time to meet the FedEx driver. He parked the truck in the back of the gallery and knocked on the door. She let him in and he rolled his dolly inside.

"Say, isn't this the place that chick was murdered?" he asked as he looked around.

"Mind your own business and just do your job," she exclaimed, annoyed at the nosy young man.

"You can start in the main room. That's where I have placed most of the large boxes and crates. Don't drop anything! This is all very expensive art, you know."

Carlota stood in the hall and watched him make several trips in and out, each time loading up the dolly and placing scanning labels on each item so they could be tracked. Once he finished, he asked her to sign for everything on a computer laptop they use. When he left, she realized it was already eleven thirty. She was nervous now about the visit from the buyer.

Carlota went into the bathroom to check her hair and put on some lipstick. Then, she walked over to the front door of the gallery and looked out to see when they drove up. She could see traffic going up and down the street. Most of it now was just people going to lunch. She was getting impatient. Being kept waiting was not one of her most favorite pastimes. She decided to go and take more of her Xanax to try to relax. She didn't think she'd taken any that morning yet, so she thought it was okay. Her body was so used to taking them by now that she was barely feeling the effects from them. They usually worked better when she accompanied them with liquor, but she didn't want to drink any alcohol. She didn't want anyone to notice the smell on her breath.

The tension in her chest became tighter. She was feeling more and more anxious when she finally heard a tap at the door.

Carlota took a deep breath and walked to the front. She put on a smile, and saw two men standing there.

"Welcome, I'm Carlota Dominguez," she said as she opened the door. Are you the gentleman from Chicago?"

"Yeah, that's me. And this is my colleague Berto Fucco," said the heavy-set man with the comb over. He looked to be about in his mid-forties, well-dressed and stylish.

"How do you do?" she said as she extended her hand to the small older man who looked to be 90 years old. He had black, round glasses that sat on the tip of his nose and he carried a bag, much like the ones doctors used to carry when they made house calls.

"Gentlemen, please come in. We're going to go into the back in my office. We can be alone there."

As they walked toward the back, the guy from Chicago explained that Mr. Fucco was an expert on detecting and authenticating art.

"I bring him along with me in cases like this. Not that we don't trust you, but we're talking about a whole lot of dough here. He's retired from the Museo D'Arte E Scieza in Florence, Italy. If you don't mind, let's take a look at the painting. Mr. Fucco is going to use an IR spectroscopic instrument that will analyze the painting."

Fucco placed his bag on Carlota's desk and opened it up. He took out a small laptop computer, and a square silver-plated gadget that had what looked like a fancy magnifying glass in the middle.

"I will need to take a very minimal sample of the canvas, if you don't mind. I'll make sure it's from an end where it won't be noticed. I'll place it here in the center of the instrument, and set it on the glass. It will allow us to examine the material and we will determine the time period it was painted in. Then, I will glide it over the painting itself, so we can examine the pigment of the paint. This won't take long."

"Of course. Let me take the painting out and put it here on the table."

Carlota opened the white mailing tube and slowly released the painting onto the work table near her desk. Mr. Fucco put on a pair of white gloves and rolled it open. Carlota's heart was racing. She couldn't wait to get his over with.

"It's magnificent, isn't it?" she exclaimed when she saw it again. "I haven't really looked at it since the night I received it. There's been a lot going on here. I didn't want to take the chance on damaging it."

"Yes, it is most beautiful," said Mr. Fucco." After looking at it a few minutes, he said, "I'm going to take just a few strands of thread from this corner here."

Fucco took a pair of pointy tweezers from his bag and carefully pulled some threads from the area he had determined would be the best for him, and not damage anything. He placed it onto the glass piece and set it on top of the computer, in a drawer where it fit perfectly. The computer lit up and began to write on the screen a bunch of symbols. Then, it stopped.

"Now, I will place it over the painting itself."

Fucco set the magnifying piece about an inch above the painting and pressed a button on the side. It lit up, and again the laptop began to read. For about two minutes, it appeared to be talking back and forth to the magnifier over the painting. Then it stopped. Fucco sat down at the table and began to type and read what the computer had analyzed.

"Well Berto, what do you say? Is it the real thing?" asked the art dealer.

"I'm afraid I have some bad news," he said, as Carlota's heart sank. "This is a very professionally done copy. But it isn't an original. The layers of oil are too thin to be of any age. And the canvas, well, that is something you can buy at any art store this day and age. I'm sorry madam, but you are in possession of a copy, not an original."

"But that can't be!" shouted Carlota. This came straight from Italy. I paid a lot of money for it."

"Whoever did this is a master of art. He has studied the detail and style of Matisse. But the product gave him away," said Fucco, shaking his head.

"Sorry, Toots. Now you know why I bring my man along wit' me. Well, I guess we'll head on back. We gotta catch the four o'clock back to New York."

As the men exited the gallery, Carlota could hardly breathe. She began to hyperventilate.

"Gustavo, it has to be Gustavo! I'll kill him!" She was screaming at the top of her voice as she ran out the back door of the gallery. She ran to her car, and was driving like a maniac back to the house. She wanted to wring his neck.

"Why? Why? I don't understand? Why?"

She pulled the car in the driveway and almost slammed it into the garage wall before putting it in park. She threw the door of the car open and ran inside. Her heart was pounding. She could feel her pulse in her temples again. She ran into the kitchen, she began to scream out his name: "Gustavo! Get your ass down here!"

Suddenly it dawned on her that his car was missing from the driveway. She ran into his studio to see if the Matisse was there. But what she found instead was an easel in the middle of the room with a large canvas on it. The writing on it said:

Carlota you Bitch, I'm leaving and you will never see me again. I hope you rot in hell!

She stood there, reading it over and over. She couldn't believe what it said. She became enraged! She ran into the kitchen and got a big butcher knife. She ran back into the studio, tearing at the canvas with all the fury she could muster. She stabbed it over and over and over, screaming at the top of her lungs. "I hate you! I hate you!"

Carlota suddenly felt a pain in her chest that stopped her in her tracks. The pain was so severe; it dropped her to her knees. She could feel a sharp stabbing pain all the way from her left arm into her chest that felt like fire. Unable to utter another word from the horrific burning that was tearing through her chest, she succumbed to the pain. She fell over onto the floor, knife still clutched in her hand. Carlota had always had a cruel heart. Now she had a still one.

34

Gustavo was awakened by the announcement over the speaker. The captain of the plane was announcing their descent into Buenos Aires. He'd slept for the whole flight. It had been the first time in a long time that he had been able to relax. After a couple of drinks, the last thing he remembered was loosening his tie and reclining his seat. Now, they were about to land.

The feeling of nervousness was starting to overtake him again. He knew that by now Carlota had found out that the Matisse was missing, and that he had double-crossed her. But he had solace in the knowing that there was nothing she could do about it. The painting couldn't be reported missing, since it had been purchased in the black market. He decided that he wasn't going to think about her ever again. His new life was about to begin. With the money from the painting, he would be able to live happily without any worries of money ever again.

The wheels of the plane touching the tarmac jolted him. He straightened out his tie and waited until the plane finished taxiing to the gate. He was seated near the front of the plane and he was anxious to get out.

Unable to reach the overhead compartment to retrieve his small carry on, the teenager seated across from him helped him get it down. The doors flew open, and it was time to leave the plane. He was nervous. Not knowing what to really expect, he just said a little prayer and moved forward slowly into the customs area.

It was a large square room with glass on the three main sides. As he reached the end of the tunnel and stepped into the room, he looked around outside at the other side of the glass. He was anxious. As he slowly made his way to the customs officer, he spotted her. She was there! Enma was there! She was even more beautiful than he remembered.

She had received the letters he had mailed Express Mail, asking her asking her to join him in Buenos Aires from Puerto Rico. That was part of his plan all along.

Gustavo had written Enma, pronouncing he had never stopped loving her and that he wanted to marry her as soon as possible. He assured her his sister would never be able to interfere in their lives ever again.

Gustavo had promised Enma that if she would give him the honor of becoming his wife, they would never have to be apart again.

Enma spotted Gustavo through the glass and waived with a big smile. Gustavo waved back. He could hardly contain himself with joy. But he still had to go through the customs process.

Hurrying to be one of the first, he looked around to find one of the older customs agents. The older ones were the ones who always seemed to be easier to bribe. Just in case, he had placed the two hundred dollar bills in his jacket pocket, so he could easily get to them if he needed to. There was an older man near the far end who looked to be the type he was looking for.

Gustavo walked up to him and greeted him in Spanish.

The man asked Gustavo to open his bag. He scanned through it quickly and spotted the tube right away. He asked Gustavo what was in it. He replied that he was an art dealer from the U.S. and was bringing a painting home to his family.

Reaching in his pocket for a business card, he handed it to the agent along with the money, folded the same size as the card as to not attract attention.

The officer opened the tube and pulled out its content. He unrolled the painting and looked at it. At first Gustavo wasn't paying much attention. He was still busy looking at Enma on the other side of the glass.

"I thought you said you had one painting. There are two paintings in here."

Gustavo thought he had heard the man incorrectly.

"Two?" he said as he looked down. It took a second for it to register. There, as well as the Matisse, was the Picasso! That's what Harry had meant when he texted he had "left a little present in the mailbox."

Victoria's Peach Pie Recipe

First, we make the crust.

You will need:
2 1/2 cups of all-purpose flour, plus a little extra for dustin'
I teaspoon of Kosher salt
3 Tablespoons of Sugah'
12 Tablespoons of unsalted butter cut into small pieces
8 Tablespoons of shortnin' (chill it first)
6-8 Tablespoons of really cold water

Put all dry ingredients in food processor. Mix. Add butter, mix.

Add the shorntnin', mix some more. Start to add cold water slowly and mixin' until it forms a ball. You may not need all of it. When it forms a ball, take it out on to a floured surface. Cut into two separate pieces. Form them into balls, flatten out into disks. Wrap in plastic wrap. Place into fridge for about half an hour.

When you are ready, roll it into two pie shapes.

The pie stuffin'

You will need:
6 cups of peeled, sliced peaches
3 Tablespoons of fresh squeezed lemon juice
The zest of one lemon
1/4 teaspoon of Kosher salt
1/2 teaspoon of Allspice
3 Tablespoons of Tapioca
About 2 tablespoons of sugah'

Mix everything and let sit in fridge for about 30 minutes until the flavors marry. Now don't skip this step y'all!

Roll out dough onto a floured surface and place in a lightly floured glass pie pan. Sprinkle bottom of pie crust with a tablespoon of sugah'

With a fork poke pie crust 4 to 5 times. Pour pie fillin' inside and cover with second pie crust.

Now cut off the extra dough and pinch it pretty. Poke 4 to 5 times on top with a fork and sprinkle with another bit of sugah'. Bake at 375 for 45 minutes.

Let it cool and enjoy Ya'll!